Will Dolores Come to Tea?

Will Dolores Come to Tea?

Elisabeth Russell Taylor

ARCADIA BOOKS
LONDON

Arcadia Books Ltd
15–16 Nassau Street
London W1N 7RE

www.arcadiabooks.co.uk

First published in Great Britain 2000
Copyright © Elisabeth Russell Taylor 2000

Elisabeth Russell Taylor has asserted her moral right
to be identified as the author of this work in accordance with the
Copyright, Designs and Patents Act, 1988.

All Rights Reserved. No part of this publication
may be reproduced in any form or by any means
without the written permission of the publishers.

A catalogue record for this book is available from the British Library.

ISBN 1–900850–39–7

Typeset in Monotype Bembo by Discript, London WC2N 4BL
Printed in the United Kingdom by The Cromwell Press, Trowbridge, Wiltshire

Acknowledgements
'The Return' is the third part of *Swann Song* (Hutchinson 1988), reprinted here by
permission of the publisher

Published with financial support of the London Arts Board

Arcadia Books distributors are as follows:

in the UK and elsewhere in Europe:
Turnaround Publishers Services
Unit 3, Olympia Trading Estate
Coburg Road
London N22 6TZ

in the USA and Canada:
Consortium Book Sales and Distribution, Inc.
1045 Westgate Drive
St Paul, MN 55114–1065

in Australia:
Tower Books
PO Box 213
Brookvale, NSW 2100

in New Zealand:
Addenda
Box 78224
Grey Lynn
Auckland

in South Africa:
Peter Hyde Associates (Pty) Ltd
PO Box 2856
Cape Town 8000

Contents

The Vacancy	1
The Wages of Virtue	21
Sabine's Version	29
The Banana-Skin Tree	46
Work	58
The Mistress	77
A Different Country	84
Charming	91
Crises. 1939	99
Will Dolores Come to Tea?	106
The Return	115
Family Relations	174

The Vacancy

JOEL STEIN was brought up by a pushy mother who had come to rather despise her dreamy loser of a husband killed in a road accident when Joel was eight. Rebecca Stein determined that her only child would get the best education in Johannesburg, whatever sacrifices that might involve her in. She took a job as a secretary in a law firm to support Joel and herself and steered Joel towards sitting scholarships. By the time he entered public school Rebecca Stein knew her son was in for great things. And being white in apartheid South Africa, with English as his first language, conferred on Joel the assurance that despite having a mother who worked, he could expect eventually to take up his rightful position at the helm of the Republic, in whatever field he chose.

I knew nothing of Joel's trajectory when I met him. A cousin of mine who was in the obstetrics department of a London teaching hospital introduced us. I was attracted to Joel on our first meeting. He had sparkling intelligence. He appeared interested in everything and hugely grateful to be in London where there was so much to see and do. He told me his intention was to stay no more than three years. But before the three years were up he and I were married.

I had no intention of living in South Africa and Joel himself was by now lukewarm about returning. He had come to the conclusion that he would rather be a large fish in a large pond than a large fish in a small pond. He was working excessively hard and long hours at the hospital and when not at work was hard at play: cricket and tennis in summer, bridge, poker and chess in winter. I liked it in him that he had a wide circle of men friends – mostly from South Africa – but I liked it less that he spent so much of our time with them. I found myself delegated to the kitchen to knock up the food and drink that were the accompaniment to each of Joel's pursuits.

After about five years the unvarying routine of our marriage was starting to depress me. Was my infertility, I wondered, triggered by that? Infertility became so central to our life that it led Joel to research the subject and eventually to make it his speciality. Both of us had taken it for granted that we would have children. Having tried for five years to become pregnant without success, I took all the tests. Only then was it revealed that one of my fallopian tubes had been severed, almost certainly during the appendectomy I had when a child.

Once we had discovered that there was no way we were going to have a family, we both rather went off sex. Joel started to give up some of his free time – his sports and games time – to work even harder. He and two South African colleagues opened a fertility clinic. They made spectacular advances in that field and although I could see that the intellectual satisfaction was paramount, I noticed too that Joel was distastefully gratified by the huge amounts of money he was making. We grew apart. In the end we divorced, but without acrimony.

I had married before I had decided what I wanted to make of myself. I thought I was marrying someone whose drive was to relieve human suffering. I had no idea that Joel had his eye on wealth – and a title.

It was at least fifteen years after we were divorced that I bumped into Joel. I had been living in France, working on a women's journal. I had come back to London and was sharing a flat with an old school friend while I searched for a place of my own. It was my friend, Sonia, who arranged for me to accompany her to a dinner party to which she had been invited.

'Are you sure your hosts will be happy with an extra woman?'

'They'll be delighted,' Sonia assured me. 'They like meeting new people.'

Sonia's only fault in my eyes was her pathological unpunctuality. However, since we were being invited to friends of hers, I did not press her to hurry while she hesitated in front of her wardrobe and her looking-glass. But on arrival at the dinner, I was rather embarrassed to see that the other guests were already seated when we were ushered into the dining-room. Our host, Sir Clapton Brown, bustled towards us and showed Sonia to a vacant seat at one end of one table and me at the end of another. He dismissed as unnecessary our apologies.

'We've only just emerged from the drawing-room ourselves,' he said reassuringly. 'But you missed out on some sensational Green Dragons and Dusky Salomes!' Sir Clapton Brown was well on in his seventies and belonged to the era of cocktail drinking.

I found myself seated on my left by a man dressed in a grey Issey Miyake jump-suit. He introduced himself to me as Gustave Lederer and admitted he didn't know a soul at the party. On my right was Justin Bouverie, who assured me we had met before. I could not remember having done so but he insisted it was the case and presumed some intimacy with me. He spoke to me as one does to an old friend.

'I don't know "sir" very well. I'm simply acting as his jobbing architect, designing the conservatory at his place outside Farringdon. I thought this was to be a little do *à trois* to discuss the planting ... There's simply acres of glass ... What a bonus to find you here, my dear! Where have you been all these years?' I told him a little – nothing too specific. It was agreeable to have someone with whom to share the pleasures of such excellent food and wine.

'This is positively Trimalchion,' Justin observed. And if there was no evidence of slaves to anoint our feet and no Daedalus to carve a pigeon from a ham bone and certainly no blowers of horns, there was a bevy of exotic-looking waitresses kitted out in short-skirted, low-bodiced black silk, each with a white silk 'pinny' at the waist. I suppressed a giggle. I was put in mind of a chorus line at the Moulin Rouge; any moment I expected the bevy to high-kick its way back to the kitchen before returning, holding aloft the umpteenth course. The waitresses were deft: the gold and silver entrée dishes, in which the food lay interred, were heavy, yet they passed from guest to guest as if timed to some unheard music. They were followed by similarly masked men dressed in black silk, whose job it was to serve the wines.

I longed to refer to Sonia. She had told me to be prepared for unusually fine food and drink and some highly eccentric company, but I was not prepared for quite what I was seeing.

The dining-room was candle-lit. I could make out the two large tables at which about eighteen guests were seated. The candles were so placed as to illumine the plates and glasses and leave the company in shadow, looking as if they had lately quit the set of a Fellini film. The rustle of silks was continuous, the heady scent of musk wafted over us as the waitresses stirred the air. I thought I could make out that one of the guests had her neck lassoed in a feather boa and another in six rows of crystal. I peered across the table and was pretty sure that the man in front of me was rouged and powdered. Conversations were being conducted in low voices, as if in secret. There was an all-pervading sense of complicit intimacy.

I mentioned to Justin my embarrassment at having been brought to such a gathering without having had a personal invitation.

'My friend just rang and said she was bringing me along!'

'Oh, don't you worry about that!' someone said, having overheard my remark. 'Clapton and Phoebe love to have new blood introduced into their thrashes. They give them every month, you know. We're always being asked to find more women. Women are much more elusive than men! There are always single men hanging about waiting for a free dinner but beautiful women are few and far between.' As he trailed off, elaborating his theme, the image of a cattle-market entered my mind. Up-market, but cattle-market none the less.

'Who are all these people?' I whispered to Justin.

'Search me!' he replied, taking a long draught of wine, 'but clearly a distinguished cross-section of *le tout Londres*. I came across a judge, a couple of MPs, a physician and some lovely ladies over drinks ... Not many couples, I'd say.' I turned to talk to Gustave Lederer who was apologizing to the Japanese woman at his left that he found the Japanese 'quite impossible to rumble'. He had been writing a tourist guide to Japan 'but I have found the European mind is incapable of excavating that of the Japanese. We don't seem to have the appropriate tools at our disposal. I'm afraid all that I've succeeded in doing is to render a very European view.' The Japanese woman tinkled with laughter. I turned back to Justin and asked him what he was designing other than the conservatory. He said he had just turned down a shopping mall *à la* Trump for a much more modestly paid day-centre for the disabled.

'I just felt life was too bloody short to go on endlessly doing things that don't matter,' he explained.

Wine was making me like better the two men between whom I was sandwiched. They were interesting and rather modest. I needed to make new friends. I had lost touch with many of my old ones. I imagined they had clung to Joel.

Coffee and liqueurs were being served at the dining tables. There was evidently to be none of that nonsense involving the women retiring and the men staying put to tell smutty stories. I was glad of it. Just as I finished my first cup of coffee and was choosing a *petit four* from a plate Justin offered me, I noticed a woman rise from her seat at the other side of the table and move across the room, between the tables. As she moved, she hitched up one side of her full skirt and tucked it into the belt at her waist. I sensed at once that she was naked under her skirt and in the flickering candlelight I saw I was right. Her pudenda was visible, grotesquely large and black as it might appear in a Freud painting. She stood so that she could be seen by as many guests as looked in her direction. She thrust her hand between her legs. In the silence that accompanied her performance, all heads turned to face her. Cups hung in the air, mouths stopped chewing. Then while she rubbed herself energetically, raised voices urged her on. Some chairs scraped the floor. Various guests rose and left the room. Simultaneously, a woman unbuttoned her blouse and from layers of black lace revealed a huge breast.

'Look here! Over this way! Look what I've got!' Some did turn and look. I panicked. How was I going to get out of this? What were Justin and Gustave thinking about it all? And then my attention was distracted and I saw that the seemingly pregnant woman with the unusually low voice, who had been sitting beside the second exhibitionist, was reassuring her that it was, indeed it was a very fine breast and deserved a great deal more attention than it was presently receiving. But as she spoke, it became clear to me that she was not a pregnant but a phallic woman, a man in drag, and that whilst he was genuinely appreciative of the generous maternal symbol, he was dangerously jealous of it.

'Come!' Justin had hold of my arm and was drawing me to my feet, indicating that we were getting out. I rose, rather bent, hoping to make myself inconspicuous.

'Not going already!' Sir Clapton Brown called from

where he was sitting. 'But the fun's only just beginning.' I was impressed by my host's manner. He was in no way put out that Justin and I were choosing to leave. Indeed, he rose and escorted us to the hall and graciously looked forward to seeing us on our next visit.

'First Saturday of the month, remember. Don't bother to confirm. I'll be expecting you.'

Just as Justin and I were about to go out into the night, I remembered Sonia. She was still at table and would certainly find it odd if I left without explanation. Justin volunteered to go back and let 'the ravishing blonde in the scarlet dress', as I described her, know that I had left for home.

I went into the front garden and sat on a bench sited under a fine Georgian lantern. It was a glorious balmy June night. All about me rose the delicious scents of dew-damp earth and jasmine. A car sped into the silence and drew up somewhere near. I heard the almost soundless close of the driver's door and registered that only very expensive cars achieve that tone. The porch gate that separated the road from the garden path swung open and a man strolled in. I could see at once that it was Joel. Tall, broad and with a slight stoop at the shoulders. I stood.

'Can it be Joel?' I heard myself enquire.

'Good heavens! Fancy meeting you!' He came towards me. Neither of us seemed to know what was the appropriate greeting in these circumstances. Should we shake hands? Kiss? Hug, even? In the event, Joel simply asked me what on earth I was doing sitting in the garden in the dark, and I told him.

'I've not seen you at the Clapton Browns' before.'

'No. This evening's the first time I've met the couple, let alone been in their house. Sonia brought me along.'

'Sonia? Sonia Grieves?'

'Yes.'

'I'm glad you've kept in touch with her.' I thought that remark patronizing, as if Joel imagined that everyone we had known together – even my old school friend – had stuck to him and it was a good thing someone had chosen to stick to me. Then Justin returned.

'Oh, and you and Justin still keep in touch!'

'Well, no, not exactly.' I explained that I had completely forgotten I had ever met Justin but had hugely appreciated his support that evening. Joel went on to say that he usually dined with the Clapton Browns in the week, as more often than not he was in the country at weekends. He knew that Clapton (as he liked to be called) held a thrash on the first Saturday of each month and asked me whether I would be going the following month. I said I didn't know but rather thought not.

'Bye!'

'Bye!'

Joel passed into the house through the door Justin had been keeping ajar for him.

During the lazy Sunday that followed, I quizzed Sonia about the goings-on at the Clapton Browns. She told me that the very mixed collection of people that gathered about 'sir' were there to satisfy *all* their appetites. 'Sex is the great leveller,' she added, saying that I would be as likely to meet a pork butcher as a politician, a mortician as psychiatrist ... And every variety of sexual preference: 'hetero, homo, trans, in pairs, in groups' but always to the accompaniment of fine food and wine. 'Phoebe prides herself on her exemplary food!' Sonia went on to say that since the house had ten bedrooms, each with its own bathroom, people could be discreet and pair off 'or four-off or whatever', according to taste, and take their pleasure behind locked doors 'unless they prefer to be watched'.

'Wasn't there a little incident at your table?' she asked.

When I explained, she said the 'poor love' was sixty if a day and inordinately proud of her endowment. 'All she wants is for it to be acknowledged. Celebrated, even. Not much to ask, one would have thought.' Sonia sounded so reasonable, so charitable. I thought it best not to comment. I did not want her to think I was disapproving. I did not want her to think I was critical. I was not. I was simply astonished to have found myself in the ante-chamber to something approaching a Roman orgy.

Sir Clapton's final exhortation 'I'll be expecting you!' rang in my ears from time to time during the month of June. I had been disturbed by their dinner-party and the complicity surrounding it, surprised by Sonia's attitude (and determined not to pry into her own reasons for frequenting the Clapton Browns), and curious as to why Joel was visiting.

I settled into a flat in South Kensington, not far from the Clapton Browns' town house in The Boltons. I was working on projects for a new magazine scheduled to appear later that year. Fortunately, being busy both with work and getting my flat in order, I did not register that I was lonely. I did however sense that I was somehow at risk, suspended between the familiarity of my old life and the unfamiliarity of my new life. But at risk from what? The Clapton Brown ménage and all that that entailed? How was it that they were so confident in assuming that everyone was on the make, or if not the make the look-out, and shared in that variety of sexual predilections? I broached this with Sonia. She said that most people took it for granted that anyone in whose company they find themselves is like them or they wouldn't be in their company. 'The Clapton Browns assume one is Conservative, prejudiced and bored and that one's sex-life is in constant need of pepping up.'

I did go back to the Clapton Browns. But had I not bumped into Joel that first night, I doubt that I would have done; I would have told Sonia that it was simply not my scene. As a journalist I was in the position of being sanctioned to coax invitations from just about anybody. I was paid to be interested in everything. Were I to find myself seated at a dinner party next to a man of looks, wealth and dazzling intelligence, there was nothing to stop me assuring him of my passionate interest in machine tools and proposing a visit to his factory. Not even his wife would regard this as a proposition. But I felt inclined neither to pursue nor be pursued.

I was, however, curious about Joel. Would his wife accompany him this time and if so, what sort of a marriage were they having? I had known Anya a long time ago, before she met Joel. I remember her saying that all the most eligible men were married but would almost certainly divorce and she was waiting for the second time round. The fact that she was bird-brained did not prevent her from knowing what she wanted and how to get it. She had never been a friend of mine, just a friend of a friend. She combined great physical beauty with a mind barely capable of memorizing a recipe for poached eggs. She had no sense of humour. I used to meet her in the company of a little crowd of women. She would sit among us, po-faced, while our rib-cages ached from laughing, enquiring what was funny and why was it funny. I remember thinking what a social liability she would be to a man had she been merely passably good-looking. As it was, she was dazzling. Not only perfectly slim but curvaceous. Even her feet and hands were perfectly proportioned. As a budding actress she eschewed modelling, regarding it as tawdry by comparison with her art. But as a woman whose tastes exceeded the resources of her purse, she allowed her feet to her charming knees and her hands to her tiny wrists to model varnish and creams, jewellery and watches. Women were envious of Anya. Men were jealous of the men with whom she kept company. In the cold light of day, I had not been surprised that Joel had settled for this trophy-woman. Their children would be stunningly beautiful, if not Nobel prize-winners. And how much time did Joel have to spend in the company of a wife, anyhow?

On the second Saturday evening I attended the Clapton Browns' dinner, there were no obvious displays of a sexual nature. From time to time during dinner guests left the table for a while and then returned, having skipped a course or two, and would make up for it by consuming tit-bits from platters of savoury and sweetmeats placed on a groaning sideboard. I was fine-tuned to what was going on around me. I was fascinated. I felt myself an extra in a drama, privileged to spend the whole evening enjoying the food and wine and some lively conversation, while all responsibility for the success of the action resided in the lead performers.

Joel and Anya arrived late but not too late to have to forego cocktails. The lime-green concoction that evening was lethal, no doubt mixed to relax newcomers. Even allowing for my double vision, there must have been fifty or sixty guests in the drawing-room when I spotted Joel and Anya. I had been drawn into a small circle at the centre of which was Gustave Lederer. He had found a few travellers like himself and they were exchanging hardships in the blasé manner of the seasoned explorer. I was struck by how frail, even ill they appeared but the one woman among them, who had single-handedly driven camels across the lower Sahara, certainly looked up to it. In other circumstances I would have got an interview from her. Then someone whose book I had once savaged in *Politics and People* tried to pick me up. Fortunately, he was too drunk to catch my name. If he had registered it I would have feared for my life. No author forgets the name of a reviewer who had been underwhelmed by his work.

As I unknotted myself from this little gathering I saw Joel nod to me in a manner that could have been mistaken for an adjustment to his shirt collar. I acknowledged his recognition but took it that Anya had not, and was not intended to. I moved back to the group of travellers to conceal myself. The author moved with me.

'My God! What on earth are you doing here?' Gustave exclaimed.

'You're not going to believe this,' the author said, 'but you see that magnificent woman?' Gustave's eyes focused on six feet of Caribbean sunshine. 'Her husband has promised me two tickets for the cup final if I let him watch me fuck his wife.'

'Your luck's in.'

'You may think so but don't laugh – I can't get a stand these days.'

'Oh the irony of it all!' Gustave heaved with laughter. I looked about and took in the magnificent chandeliers, period furniture and old masters. The words 'bordello', or even 'house of ill-repute' did not spring to mind. This was the perfect foil of a setting for the dramas being enacted.

'...He went into the law because he recognized his own criminal tendencies. He chose to be a solicitor because it brings him in daily contact with crime but allows him to earn as much if not a bloody lot more than his clients and keeps him most of the time in safety behind his own bar. He likes a drink, you know, does Herbert...' Mr Simon Potts, MP for a small constituency in the shires, was addressing another MP. What, I wondered, would the Tory ladies of the market town where Mr Potts had recently acquired a charming constituency house feel about their man if they knew the company he kept in London and these details about his campaign manager?

A table plan was prominently displayed in the hall and guests were ushered in its direction to consult it. I found myself seated between a forty-something Irishman who said he was in the meat business, and a much younger Italian, a window-dresser at Liberty's. I asked the Italian how he had met the Clapton Browns and he told me Phoebe had visited the store wishing to buy a piece of furniture he had used to dress a window. He had been called to remove the said piece of furniture and replace it with something else, and they had got talking. I did not ask the meat man how he had got himself involved with the Clapton Browns. I had the feeling he might ask me to mind my own business. He was physically intimidating, very obviously someone with a past, present and future, all of which rang of crime and violence and the loyalty of a good woman. I talked to him about Ireland and horses over the hors-d'œuvres. He proposed that we go for a stroll before the fish course but I declined. I had begun to be charmed by his voice and his assurance, but I did not want to be observed moving away from the table towards a conclusion everyone watching could predict. But that was not all. I did not want Joel to see me compromised.

I only became conscious of the background music when it stopped and a sort of musical chairs ensued. Guests were removing to other place settings to meet people they did not know and to catch up with those they did know. That evening the Clapton Browns had brought into the dining-room seven small tables, seating eight at each, instead of the two huge ones of the previous month. I sat tight and felt an arm being tugged by Joel who had taken the Irishman's place. The vacated places at our table filled and Joel held court. Once he had got the whole table talking, he turned to me and asked me a few questions about where I was living – and with whom. I answered with a half-smile, nothing more. We were both occupied eating. Joel did not face me while he spoke. Eventually, he rose to his feet.

'Let's talk outside. I can't hear myself think.' I don't know why I followed him out of the dining-room. Others had got up from their tables and were standing drinking in the library and on the stairs. Someone was playing a piano and singing 'Is That All There Is?'. Joel grabbed my hand and, pushing through a group talking on the stairs, led me up into a bedroom heavy with oak and damask and the scent of datura. I was confused, not thinking, avoiding thinking, about what was happening, conscious of this being a man's room, a man used to Havana cigars, a gun at his shoulder, a wig on his head...

I blamed what happened on drink at the time. Joel's rough handling, his savage assault shocked me. Perhaps I remembered that this was not like him, but I was not conscious of thinking that. He did not woo me. He did not remove my clothing or his. He simply unzipped, drew up my skirt, pushed me across the bed with my legs dangling over the side and in no more than it took to swear at me – call me a slut and a whore crying out to be taken – we both came. Then Joel left without a further word. I was stunned.

I need not have felt embarrassed as I came down the stairs. No one noticed me. No one asked where I had been when I resumed my place at table – nor where the man next to me had gone. I felt flushed. Did they think I had left the table to 'powder my nose', or did they know it was to be shagged by my ex-husband? I pulled myself together and joined in the conversation at the table. It was political and involved contention. I knew I was liable to become partisan and rude. I thought the best plan would be to leave the house. I got up and went first to whisper to Phoebe that I was leaving. We spoke for a few minutes, arranging to meet for lunch. I regained my cool and wandered into the hall, where Joel was helping Anya into a wrap. I saw that Anya was pregnant.

'Do you remember Claudia?' Joel asked his wife, all the while keeping his eyes on me.

'Oh yes, we met somewhere ... long time ago' Anya

replied dreamily. 'How are you? Still doing clever things?'
'Yes,' I agreed.
'I'm having a baby!' she told me unnecessarily.
'You must be delighted.'
'Of course.'
'I expect you're doing all the exercises...' I tried.
'I go to the gym every day.' I was sure she would: Anya would always tend her body with a degree of commitment she would never think to apply to her mind.

Was I jealous of Anya? Did I wish I were pregnant with Joel's child? Did I want that lonely routine, rattling about in a huge house while an absent husband lavished his attentions on the problems of other women all day, and played sport and games with his friends in the evenings and at weekends, with the occasional foray into the outside to pursue sexual partners? I did not. It was impossible to feel jealous of the beautiful, vacuous Anya who, come to think of it, was not all that beautiful any longer. Her skin had become puffy and lined. Her hair had thinned. She carried her body uneasily, the unborn child held high above what had been her tiny waist.

Not everybody invited to the Clapton Browns' came for sex. No doubt if they accepted an invitation more than once they must have realized what went on and how, if they so wished to take advantage themselves, there were opportunities so to do. But no pressure was brought to bear one way or the other. Sometimes there arose an incident of unmissable exhibitionism that offended more of the company than were aroused by it. But no one would do anything to intervene. I rather enjoyed the theatre the transvestites created, but then they were out to entertain whereas exhibitionists have only themselves in mind.

I got to know Phoebe quite well. I liked her; she was eccentric and had a sharp wit. I never got to know why it was she wanted to be the queen of London's fashionable sex parties. As for 'sir', I found him unfathomable. He confined himself to the duties of ringmaster and paymaster. He never participated in any sexual activity so far as I could make out. Maybe that accounted for Phoebe's insatiable interest in everyone else's sex life – and her appetite for very young men. Phoebe and I would occasionally meet for lunch at her preferred watering holes, Harrods or Fortnums, where she was treated to a great deal of bowing and scraping. I imagine her account must have been valuable to both stores. We never discussed her parties in any detail. Once or twice she said how pleased she was that I seemed to get on so well with 'that nice doctor'. She never found out what the 'nice doctor's' and my past relationship had been.

I met men I would rather have come to know under different conditions. There were two members of the House of Lords, well known for their espousal of human rights issues, to whom I used to talk. One was an historian. I bumped into him and his wife in different circumstances and obeyed the unwritten law that one never acknowledged previous acquaintance if it had been at the Clapton Browns. Sometimes I would notice someone in the bar at the theatre and feel I knew them from somewhere or other but could not place them. I always veered on the safe side and waited to be acknowledged first. I became furtive and secretive.

I was working full out. My work took me all over England interviewing, researching local issues in local libraries, visiting country hotels to find out the sort of reception accorded to single women. I had no time to establish a social life. Joel and I slipped into the habit of Saturday nights at the Clapton Browns and when these became more frequent, we attended. Anya accompanied Joel just twice before the birth of her son and on neither occasion did her presence in the dining-room do anything to prevent Joel meeting me upstairs. By now he had discovered he was not altogether the man he had thought he was – dutiful and tender, sensitive and affectionate – but someone in whom resided a coarse masculinity. My married experience of Joel had been of his predictability. On reflection, there had been something about his lovemaking that owed as much to passion as painting to numbers does to works of art. There were aspects of intimacy he never explored. Perhaps it had been his fastidiousness as a young doctor, perhaps it was his professional relationship with the orifices of a woman' body that prevented his mouth and fingers exploring my body. But the way he took me now, as a stranger, was altogether different. Selfish, gross and more honest for that. He was driven physically. There was no love involved, no commitment to anything but sexual arousal and gratification: need and its fulfilment. And in this depersonalized sex, sex which had nothing to do with strengthening sentimental ties, reproduction, appeasement or punishment, I too felt a sort of release. Our sessions were short. We maintained the roles of stranger to one another. I was the slut, accused of keeping my soul in my cunt. He was the commandant. How many lovers did I have? What did I do for them? Was there anything I did for them that I was not doing for him? If so, what and why? And so on. He never kissed me on the mouth; that would have dissolved the spell. He kept his kisses for his chaste wife. If only he had had more time, he would have paid men to fuck me while he watched.

We never returned to our old roles. We never discussed the past. Our old roles had separated us and led us to divorce. Our new roles were making us indispensable to one another. Neither of us had ever experienced such satisfying sex. We wanted more and more. I felt sure that whereas Joel could be unfaithful to his wife, any wife, he could never be unfaithful to the wife-mistress. But in my role as whore, Joel would threaten that were I not to go along with his deviousness he would immediately find some other whore who would.

'The world's chock-full of whores!' Joel rejoiced.

We took a small flat in Wimpole Street, just round the corner from his clinic. There I became the call-girl he telephoned and for whose services he paid. My obligation was to fit him in between the hordes of regulars he invented for me. The last thing Joel wanted was fidelity and chastity. Those qualities were the ultimate turn-offs. Despite his avowed need for a slut and a whore, I secretly remained faithful to Joel. But my mien must have altered because I noticed I was constantly being solicited in the street. My body language must have changed in response to Joel's fantasy.

'If I'd known then what I know about you now,' Joel said one day, 'I would never have let you go. I would have kept you prisoner.'

I felt chilled. I could have become one of those terrifying news stories in which women are discovered in sadomasochistic relationships darker than the dungeons in which they are concealed, stronger than the chains that bind them physically.

The slut Joel accused me of being was the person I became with him. I was indifferent to him as a person. His presence could even be an irritation. While he had intercourse with me, or we were engaged in some sort of arousal, I had no reason to consider him, only the pleasure I was deriving from his attentions, for in using me as he did, I *was* pleasured. Once he had taken what he wanted he left quickly. Looking back, I think it must have posed a problem to him to impose his fantasy on me when he was not in a state of arousal. Unlike me, Joel was never analytical. Whereas I did think about what we were doing when I was on my own, I do not believe he gave it a second thought. I was simply not there when I was not present; I was the role in which he had cast me, nothing more.

Of course, it had to happen. Someone saw us together

leaving Wimpole Street one afternoon. Joel had signalled to a passing taxi, had opened the door for me and was telling the driver where to take me. A doctor friend, who had known us when we were married, asked him, 'Wasn't that Claudia? How is she these days?' Joel was suddenly brought to his senses (as he put it to me). He felt so ghastly about years of unfaithfulness to Anya, he went home with a suitably expensive present for her and told her the truth. He did not tell her the half of it, however. He tried to placate her by pointing out how it was somehow much less of an infidelity having a relationship with an ex-wife than it might have been had he chosen someone new. Anya was not persuaded. This did not tally with her idea of what was due to her. Although I was never privy to her deepest reasons for insisting on a divorce, I think the fact that she took off for New York and the Hampshires suggests that she had planned the next stage in her life and was only waiting for Joel to provide her with the excuse and the money. She probably kicked herself when she heard later that Joel had been knighted.

I stopped going to the Clapton Browns and I kept my telephone on the answering machine. Phoebe and I lunched from time to time. She remarked that she missed me and 'that nice doctor' at the Boltons. I said we were not seeing one another any more. She tried to persuade me to come and meet new people. There was no question of that. I had no appetite for it. If I were to meet a new man I would not like the relationship to be tainted by the Clapton Browns' set-up.

Since being back in London from my years in France, I had had no time to make new friends. I had acquaintances made in connection with my work. I was forty-two when I returned, not a propitious time in life for making friends. My relationship with Joel as his fantasy whore had fully satisfied my sexual needs. And Joel, with his extraordinary self-confidence and assured place in society, provided me with a feeling of security that no new man was likely to do. Joel's telephone calls became increasingly frantic and in the end, some ten months after his divorce and Anya's departure, I returned his call. Would I meet him for dinner?

I suggested lunch. Noon tends to be less charged with promise. Throughout the period of our peculiar sexual relationship, we had never dined or lunched together in a restaurant. We never went away together. We had not spoken *à deux*, but only as strangers making conversation at the Clapton Browns'. And that is rather how we spoke together at Claridges when we met for the last time.

Joel asked me to marry him again.

'I know now how to do it,' he said.

I declined his proposal.

'But why?' I was not altogether sure I could say why without hurting him. I knew I would be bored as his wife because I knew that as his wife he would revert to treating me as he had during our marriage – and as, no doubt, he had treated Anya. Wives were a particular category of woman ... Added to which, Joel was so rich by then, so famous, and knighted into the bargain, I knew I would find the lifestyle he had elaborated anathema. Which was not to say I disliked him or lacked respect for his achievements. His previous assertion that had he known about me what he had subsequently discovered, he would never have agreed to a divorce, I knew to be as unlikely as I would have wished it to be. Joel needed two women. I had preferred and was better at being the 'other'.

It was another rich knight of the realm who with boundless self-confidence, energy and self-love opined that once a man marries his mistress a vacancy is created. This was not the final irony I was willing to allow to befall me.

The Wages of Virtue

I FOUND MY SEAT on the front row of the amphitheatre just as the house lights dimmed. Unfortunately I had to disturb a dozen members of the audience to reach it. This flustered me and I took particular care not to upset anyone further while I removed my coat. Nor did I look to see who was sitting either side of me.

Only minutes into the first soprano aria I became vaguely aware of an arm outstretched at my right. At first I did not grasp that it was intended to attract my attention. Then, gradually, it dawned on me that my neighbour wanted to borrow my opera glasses. Without taking my eyes off the stage, I passed the cord over my head and handed the glasses to my right. Moments later, however, I wanted them back. A much-vaunted tenor making his début at Covent Garden had appeared and I wanted a close-up. I held out my arm. My neighbour ignored it. Now, I felt irritated; instead of being able to give the opera my full attention, I was dividing it between the action on stage and the action into which I was being personally corralled. But I was not going to insist; I can't bear noise in the auditorium during a performance. Eventually, my neighbour thrust the glasses back under my nose and I forgot my earlier irritation.

As soon as the curtains closed on the first act, I was aware that whoever had been seated at my right was pushing a path through the row to her right in the direction of the bar and the Ladies. She was evidently old, not so much wearing her dull brown-grey overcoat as wrapped in it, as if in a blanket, her head concealed in a wool hood. Over her shoulder she lugged a shopping bag. How wrong, I thought, to judge an opera devotee from appearances.

I spent the interval reading the programme notes. *The Wages of Virtue* had only recently come to light and this was its first performance in England. It was the work of a little-known German baroque composer who had hitherto been thought to have confined himself to religious music. At the heart of *The Wages of Virtue* I discerned an almost indecent erotic fervour. The heroine's passion for her lord, and her spiritual marriage to him portrayed in the first act, produced music of such soaring intensity I could only fear the depths to which the composer would propel us in the second act, when his heroine trades spiritual fulfilment for corporeal satisfaction. Such powerful masochism combined with retribution attaches to the outcome of the narrative, I thought the opera merited a health warning.

Not long into the second act, the old woman extended her arm and, when I did not react immediately, nudged me. Although I was not happy about sharing my glasses, I couldn't find reasonable grounds to refuse. (Did I not expect my neighbours to share their garden shears?) I was annoyed, not only because I wanted to be free to use the glasses at a second's notice myself, but because I had started to argue with myself as to the old woman's right to make the demand of me. On the one hand: she's taking too much for granted, they're mine! On the other: I'm selfish, I'm ungenerous. Of course, I handed them over. But when sometime later I extended my arm, she did not respond. When I realized she was not going to relinquish the glasses I became anxious: would I *ever* get them back?

I did. She left her seat at the second interval, having silently deposited the glasses in my lap when the lights went up. I secured the cord round my neck and turned to watch her battle her way along the row, her shopping bag bumping into every knee in her path. I noticed how she was examined with curiosity, even distaste.

Instead of immersing myself in the programme notes, I found myself making a mere eye-reading. I was distracted by an internal debate: if in Act Three I refused to share my glasses with the old woman, would she turn nasty and create a scene? And if I did share them, could I be certain she would return them? Why was I making such a production of the matter? Was it because the glasses had sentimental value? Or was it because they would cost more than I could afford to replace?

I had inherited the glasses from my father. They were all he had had to leave me. He had been a sessions violinist and had introduced me to opera when I was a child. The glasses had come to symbolize the far-sightedness he had in educating me in something that would fill me with pleasure long after he was no longer there to share in it.

I found the libretto of the third act difficult to follow, despite my fluency in German. The heroine indulges in such sophisticated casuistry to justify her revelation regarding the indivisibility of passion that I needed to listen more closely than look. So, too, did the old woman. She didn't extend her arm until the final immolation. I acquiesced.

The curtain fell; the audience rose. Amid thunderous applause the cast took curtain call after curtain call. Flunkies hauled huge bouquets of exotic flowers on stage. In response to the audience's demands, the conductor leapt from the pit to join the cast and the soprano drew an orchid from her bunch to crown their embrace. The amphitheatre expressed itself in the unbridled enthusiasm normally associated with Italian houses. I, too, was caught up in the excitement. I felt elated. That was why I didn't notice that the old woman, far from joining in the frenzy, was actually fleeing it. By the time I spotted her she was half-way up the gangway. Quickly, I gathered up my things and, regardless of the embarrassment of having to force a path through an audience determined not to have their view of a single curtain call obscured, managed to get down the stairs into Floral Street in time to spot the old woman turning right into Bow Street.

Bow Street was in chaos. Half the street was up and parking restricted. The police were waving on taxis but allowing private limousines to wait with their engines running. Animal Rights protesters massed behind barricades. Tall men with confident voices, one arm held aloft, stood in the pool of light cast by the chandeliers in the foyer, hoping to attract the attention of their chauffeurs. Tall women, undeterred by the threat from paint pots, hugged their furs about them and in equally loud voices proclaimed where they expected to dine. A party atmosphere prevailed. No one appeared bothered by the gate-crashers, the animal lovers and the beggars who hung around in the shadows, hoping to benefit from the generosity great musical experience was presumed to induce.

I lost sight of my quarry and panicked, worried she might have turned into an unlit alley. Was she heading for the shelter of a shop front and a cardboard box, with a sleeping bag? Or to a hostel? It would be reassuring if it were the latter. She would have a roof over her head and I could rely on a warden tactfully separating his client from my property.

Once I emerged from the crowd, I could see the old woman making her way south down Bow Street. I was not going to call after her and demand my glasses back. I was not going to stop her in her tracks and wrench them from her. Any action that brought us face to face would undoubtedly frighten her; she would misunderstand, react violently or crumble with heart failure. I was pretty sure she was unaware of what she had done. Perhaps she was a kleptomaniac; perhaps to survive she had to retrieve whatever she found and had just got used to so doing?

The crowd thinned towards Wellington Street. A few

pedestrians, searching for a restaurant, had to drop into the gutter and circle the old woman doggedly occupying the middle of the pavement. When they turned into a brasserie there was no one left between me and my quarry. She was slowing down, shuffling, dragging her shopping bag behind her. I stood still. Was she going to turn right into the Strand to join the homeless? Painfully slowly, she struggled to the zebra crossing and with effort raised her head to peer up at the lights. When they allowed, she picked her way across the Strand to a bus stop in Aldwych.

I followed. I waited at a little distance from her. I noticed how she relied on her ears to alert her to the arrival of her bus.

I sat some seats behind her but kept her within my sights. I could see she was having difficulty excavating her shopping bag. I assumed she was looking for her pass among what might be all her worldly goods.

'Lost y'r pass? Put your specs on, grandma!' the conductor advised, adding that he hadn't got all night and where was she going, anyhow? I didn't hear her reply. The conductor demanded ninety pence and on his return down the aisle felt free to complain loudly of 'bloody foreigners'. 'Foundry Road!' he called out, determined no doubt to ensure the old woman would not be taking further advantage of the patience of London Transport.

Foundry Road typified those used by documentary film makers to illustrate the perfidy of the past twenty years' housing policy: once sturdy Victorian houses neglected by absentee landlords and local councils alike. Front yards dumps for discarded mattresses, wheelless prams and bicycles, smashed lavatory pans and bursting plastic bags of stinking household waste.

The front door of number five swung open on broken hinges. The entrance was barely lit by a twenty-watt bulb. I followed the old woman, careful not to be seen or heard. But I need not have bothered. She was oblivious to me. She pushed at a door to one side of the hall and shuffled in. I waited. I was becoming accustomed to the semi-darkness and noticed that the stairs to the upper floors had been partitioned off. The words 'Palace Squat' had been scrawled in ill-controlled letters across the plasterboard wall.

Having given the old woman time to put down her bag and feel safe within her four walls, I knocked quietly on her door. No response. I knocked a little louder. Eventually she pulled open the door and peered out.

'I think you have my opera glasses,' I suggested, careful that my voice betrayed no menace. She looked up at me, uncomprehending. 'You borrowed them this evening, at the opera.' While she appeared to be considering this, I eased myself into her room. She had kept her coat on but taken off the wool hood. I saw she was all but bald. 'Perhaps you popped the glasses into your shopping bag?' I suggested, eyeing the bag that lay on the table. While she considered this, I looked about the room. There were two shelves, on one of which stood a gas ring and on the other a few books and photographs. I could make out German classics and opera libretti. The photographs showed men in Homburgs and women snug in fox collars. In one corner of the room lay a mattress and blankets, in the other a heap of old clothes.

The old woman sat down at the table. Sighing deeply, she removed her shoes and socks and massaged her feet. Then she rose and in her confusion brushed against the wall, dislodging a white stick. I knew then that she must be registered blind, but with enough residual sight to manage in the near-dark. I watched her creep from the room. I waited. I heard a lavatory cistern drain. Then, shockingly, pop music exploded from Palace Squat overhead. Feet were beating to the din and the ceiling shuddered. My God! What hell! Piercing cold, dirt, destitution – and now cacophony.

She was back, stretching across the table towards her bag. Was she going to retrieve the glasses? My spirits rose, for when she withdrew her hand from the depths of the bag, the cord to my glasses appeared. But it was a bread roll she extracted. She sat back, seemingly satisfied, and crumbled it and fed herself small pieces.

Now I knew that my glasses were definitely in the shopping bag. I stretched forward and removed them. They were sticky, smeared with something greasy. From force of habit, I took out my handkerchief and polished the lenses. 'I'll be going now,' I said, but the din drowned my voice. I made towards the door but found myself ineluctably forced to stop and retrace my steps. I stood in front of the old woman and passed the cord round her neck and placed the glasses in her lap. Taking both her hands in mine, I folded them round my inheritance.

Sabine's Version

It was some years after the trial that I learned that my husband – as part of his therapy, it transpired – had published a book purporting to be a factual account of his career and the events that led to his incarceration. I was suspicious from the start. My husband is virtually illiterate, quite incapable of stringing together anything more complex than a grocery list. I might never have stumbled on *I is Another* had the press not tracked me down one August, the 'silly season'. Someone got in touch with one of the tabloids and revealed the whereabouts of the wife of the once celebrated chef at Les Coteaux, presently diagnosed paranoid schizophrenic and sentenced to life in a hospital for the criminally insane for his repeated attempts on the life of his wife.

Ten years ago and the press would not have bothered with our story. But in more recent times, chefs from celebrated restaurants (and ours had four stars) have come to occupy a very special place in the nation's heart. The glossies took us up. Articles appeared in food magazines in which recipes from the restaurant were simplified for home use. *Vogue* featured my wardrobe, the *Observer* my Swiss canton, Vaud, because it was mine. *Tatler* photographed our classic Hispane Suisse. Then rather against his better judgement my husband did a series on television which gave him a sort of notoriety among a public that could never have afforded the prices we charged at Les Coteaux. I should have realized that we had had altogether much too much success and too much coverage of that success for the gossip columns not to be holding their collective breath for 'Chef' to fall from grace. And, my goodness, with what thoroughness he fell, and with what enthusiasm the press fell upon us both.

There was only one course of action for me to take and I took it. I left the country. I made no arrangements for my mail to be forwarded. Indeed, I went to some inconvenience to ensure no one knew where I was to be found. I was in no mood to be pursued.

The letter from Dr Auerbach, the psychiatrist I had arranged for Antoine to see at the outset of his crisis, had been lying on my doormat for months before I got back to London. The doctor wanted me to make an appointment to come along and see him. I was not keen to accede to this. I felt a greater need than ever to shed the past, not recover it. But because what had happened to me was the result of Antoine's illness, not any malevolence on his part, I felt obliged to acquiesce. Dr Auerbach was right in believing that the information he wanted about Antoine was something he could not obtain anywhere else.

He received me cordially. He assumed, he said, that I would be grateful to know that the asylum in which Antoine had been placed finally was not uncomfortable, not institutional in appearance nor punitive in its regime. It was sited on an island off the north coast of Scotland; since there was no means of escape from the place, the patients enjoyed a peculiar freedom. Antoine had opportunities to maintain his physical well-being with rambles in the hills, swimming in the river, even riding. These pursuits being open to him for the first time in his life, I registered more than a hint of irony in his having had to lose his mind to gain some physical gratification. But Dr Auerbach went on to say that Antoine's particular derangement was one that often produced severe effects on the heart and such patients tended not to live as long as they otherwise might. No doubt he said this to reassure me. To some extent it did. Not that I wished Antoine dead, nor that I had any plans to remarry in that event. It was simply that I felt Antoine and I had already gone through enough. I wanted to be shot of it all. Moreover, I knew that whatever the positive advantages of the facilities at Riverside (the asylum), Antoine could never be happy. No one as anxious as he could experience contentment. He would be frightened of the horses – frightened he would be thrown, trampled on, or that he would do them harm. He would be terrified that the gentle river in which he dared immerse himself would transform itself into a raging torrent and drive him downstream into the sea. He would be apprehensive in the hills, believing that the mists would fall and the ground turn to ice, that he would lose his footing and, blinded by swirling cloud, would perish undiscovered. One might say, and Dr Auerbach allowed, Antoine was frightened of his own shadow. Added to which, he understood he was imprisoned, that this was no vacation. His return ticket was not only open-ended, but subject to the vicissitudes of lawyers, doctors and civil servants.

Dr Auerbach, elaborating on the treatment Antoine was undergoing, mentioned that Riverside enjoyed an input from the Schlesinger-Shade movement that encourages the use of the arts in the programme. It was then that I discovered how *I Is Another* came to be written and published. Antoine had been 'facilitated' by one of the arts therapists. I told Dr Auerbach just how annoyed I had been by the portrait painted of me in that book. Dr Auerbach dismissed my objections as irrelevant. The function of the book had been to focus Antoine's aggression. In this it had succeeded. His experience had been profoundly painful and he had felt used. Used! By whom? Well, if I 'used' Antoine it was to further his celebrity. Surely, I should be *commended* for registering his extraordinary talent and supporting it? No one else had stepped forward. I was not going to allow the doctor to proceed to render me responsible for the violence I had endured from my husband. It was one thing for me to wish Antoine well cared for, comfortable and content; it was quite another to accept myself as the author of my victimization.

Dr Auerbach wanted to know how it had come about that Antoine and I married. The differences in our milieux and educational backgrounds appeared unbridgeable. On the face of it we were deeply unsuited. True, we shared a professional interest, but had I not realized that this was hardly sufficient heat with which to forge an intimate relationship? While the doctor spoke, I was wondering whether I should frankly admit to him that I had never intended an intimate relationship with Antoine. That I had merely recognized his culinary skill and how it might combine with my own ambition to create and run a restaurant. I decided against revealing anything of myself to Dr Auerbach. I had not contracted to attend the meeting for personal interrogation and confession but to assist the medical team in their understanding and hence their treatment of Antoine. Clearly, were I to admit to having been the least manipulative, Dr Auerbach would want to pursue the matter to its source and this was something I was not going to allow.

I took up the reins and clutched them firmly. Antoine, I explained, made his name replicating *la grande cuisine française*. This he did with unswerving accuracy. I tipped him into his frenzy by suggesting, in all good faith, that with his immaculate skills he should be inventing dishes of his own. I thought this would encourage, even flatter him. I had not realized at the time the extent to which he was devoid of imagination and confidence, and dependent on the minutest of instructions. I did not understand then that he did not have the self-esteem for such praise to enhance, but merely to perturb.

Dr Auerbach did not know that my husband had not been christened Antoine but Reg, a designation of which he was ashamed. Reg was bad enough but Reggie, favoured by those in the kitchens in which he worked as a young man, was intolerable to him. Shortly before we married he asked me to please address him as Antoine, after his dear dead master Carême. I agreed to do so in private; in public I would always refer to him as 'Chef'. The doctor was bored by this intelligence but I insisted it was significant, for when I called out to my husband 'Antoine!', and he turned to face me from his permanently stooped attitude, he always straightened his back and assumed a more confident stance. From being Reg he *became* Antoine Carême. So devoted an acolyte, he would rather have fallen on a Sabatier knife than taken shortcuts with his master's recipes, or adapted any one of them to suit contemporary taste. Every time he heard himself addressed 'Antoine' it reinforced in him a sense of his being Carême's incarnation.

I had the best intentions as regards Antoine and his career. Of course, I was benefiting from his skills, but that did not mean I treated him as a work-horse. And who knows? If Antoine had not found me he might still be working as a sous-chef in a hotel, hardly the environment for a man of near-genius. No, not at all. I knew that success in his chosen career was the one thing that might provide Antoine with fulfilment and some degree of happiness. I admit, I made a serious mistake insisting to him that his technical skills were such that he should create a style of cooking of his own, rather than endlessly recreate that of *la grande cuisine*. But I could not have calculated that this idea would sweep Antoine into a frenzy of insecurity. Perhaps I lacked psychological insight. But is that reason enough for my husband's violence towards me? Was I responsible for his warped accusation that I was 'Separating me from my master! Carême has guided me all the way along my path and now you want me to betray him!' I think not. The seeds of Antoine's madness lay deep. I had no means of identifying them before they sprouted above ground.

Dr Auerbach showed me no sympathy. He did not want

to listen to my defence. He appeared suspicious of me and rather implied that behind my account of life with Antoine lay more than I was prepared to reveal. Indeed, there was. But nothing of what he might have suspected. And because he was prying into *my* thoughts and feelings – rather than those of Antoine – and because I was determined not to disclose anything relating to my personal history, I decided not to keep further appointments with him.

∞

The principle reason for my marriage to Antoine, an uneducated foreigner with exceptional culinary skills, was that my father approved it. On the one hand, Antoine was no threat to him. On the other, he wanted me to live outside Switzerland. He liked Antoine's willingness to learn from him. I doubt that he would have wanted him as a son, but found him acceptable as a disciple.

My mother died when I was twelve. I had been fond of her but not as attached to her as I was to my father. Her death had the effect of confining Father to the château to oversee my upbringing as much as to the vault in the park. For a long while he mourned. He could not talk about Mother. Then when I was about fifteen his mood lightened a little and in addition to the interest he was showing in my education, he started to guide me to wear colours Mother had preferred and to bob my hair in the manner Mother had bobbed hers. He unlocked her jewellery from the safe and chose small brooches and fragile necklaces he thought suitable for me to wear on special occasions. He allowed me into Mother's dressing-room, unlocked the cupboards and urged me to choose from bags and scarves I liked. I noticed how glad he was when anyone suggested I resembled Mother physically, or how closely my manners reminded them of hers.

I do not remember it having crossed my mind that I was rather too old to sit on Father's lap at fifteen. Because Father had always been demonstrative with his affections, I took his behaviour for granted and enjoyed our closeness. Sometimes, he would excuse our proximity by poring over a book with me and making such an occasion the opportunity to kiss my neck and run his fingers through my hair and call me his 'pretty girl'. When I noticed that something flaccid was becoming hard between his thighs, I was neither shocked nor troubled.

His interest in what I wore involved his taking me to Paris during my school holidays and buying me lovely clothes from the leading fashion houses. He argued that the shops in Lausanne did not stock what he wanted for me; but on reflection, I can see how impossible it would have been for him to have supervised my wardrobe so closely in what was, after all, a very provincial town. The Château d'Allouette lay some six miles from the centre of Lausanne. Father was well known throughout Vaud. Had it emerged that he not only picked out my dresses but accompanied me into the changing-room, the Swiss would have been horrified, would have regarded his behaviour as utterly improper, and gossiped.

When Father suggested that I should not ruin the supple flow of silk or muslin dresses and skirts by wearing anything under them, I concurred. I liked the sensation myself. So that when he caught my breast in his hand, caressed it and told me I was beautiful, I glowed with satisfaction. And when he explored under my skirt to pleasure me, I understood what he was doing and welcomed it. I felt safe with him. Everything he did I knew was for my benefit. I knew he loved me. Utterly. There was no one whose company I would have rather kept.

I do not remember precisely when it was that Father completed my initiation. He must have led up to it imperceptibly, yet when one night he knocked on my bedroom door, entered, sat down at the foot of my bed, I am sure, looking back, that I was unconsciously prepared for what was to come. He asked me gently, sweetly even, whether I would agree to his sharing my bed. He said it was something he had been waiting for years to ask, waiting until the moment he felt I was old enough. Once I had thrown back the covers to welcome him, to reveal myself naked, I learned he had been planning to make love to me since I was a child. Would I agree to it now? I was sixteen.

He was a tender master. In those early days of our intimacy we vied with one another in contriving how best to please the other intimately and yet more passionately. We luxuriated in every aspect of sensuality. Father plied me with aphrodisiacs. I bathed and massaged him in fragrant oils.

Father maintained a largish staff within the château and there were two gardeners and their assistants in the park. Without his warning me of our need to be discreet, I understood that it was critical. It is a commonplace that servants nourish themselves on tittle-tattle. Any suggestion of Father's and my intimacy would have provided a banquet.

I felt no guilt in our being lovers, but Father did. After I married, he wrote to me asking for my forgiveness. I reassured him that I felt only gratitude for the rapturous experiences that had been my introduction to sex. But without my making the accusation, I allowed myself to imply that if he was liable for any guilt it should be for the part he played in precipitating my marriage. I wonder now what had made me write to him as I did. I only did so once. Not long after, he died. I had known his death was imminent.

Not surprisingly, he had been jealous of the young men who played court to me in Lausanne. Because there was comparatively little organized entertainment in the form of theatre, opera and so on in our provincial town, social life was hectic between families and conducted in the large houses outside town and in their parks. There were balls, parties, regattas and expeditions into the mountains. Society in and around Lausanne was something of a closed circuit: we all knew one another and a new face from as far off as Geneva (*sic*) was quickly remarked and assimilated. Many of the young men who called for me and accompanied me in the evenings were fellow students at the university. Father knew their families. He could not show himself rude or inhospitable, but he did rather give way to a tendency to crush these young men with his scholarship in arcane subjects. Not one of them was good enough for me. Then, since they were all Swiss, he would say no Swiss was good enough for me, that they were to a man chauvinist and would curtail my every effort to achieve for myself. I must marry an Englishman or an American and live in the English language – so much richer in possibilities than the French!

It was not unusual in those days for a young woman in Switzerland to be a virgin on her wedding night and I found it easy to field and adroitly pass such intimate approaches as a few young Swiss men dared make. However, I noticed that I was attracting bolder advances from the fathers of these men, advances much more troublesome to deflect. I must have been unconsciously radiating some of the scent of experience.

Ever since Mother died, Father and I spent my school holidays together. Father wanted me to get used to travel and toured me through the museums, churches and archaeological sites throughout Europe. I owe my education, my taste and my enthusiasms much more to my father than any institution of learning. Father said he wanted to introduce me to every possibility so that I would be truly in a position to make choices. He was delighted in my growing determination to become a restaurateur, a decision conceived in his library among his books and with him *in situ*.

For those who never visited Les Coteaux, I should perhaps

mention that this was no ordinary restaurant. We occupied a unique position in London – indeed, in the world. For one thing, we were awarded four stars for 'Chef's' cuisine. Our produce was grown especially for us and our meat was supplied from herds we controlled ourselves. Our cellar was considered the finest in London. In addition to the more obvious side of Les Coteaux, we also had study facilities for students of gastronomy. Papers were written funded by us and researched with the help of our library. We became the centre of the history of food, eating and cookery in Europe. Antoine had nothing whatever to do with the academic side of Les Coteaux. Indeed, sometimes I wondered whether he ever fully took in what it was I was organizing. From time to time I managed to get him to cook from Apicius or from Jane Austen for a literary society, but although he agreed somewhat unenthusiastically, he never fully understood the role these societies were playing in our celebrity.

Looking back over my relationship with Antoine, and having to face the part I played in his terrible fate, I am obliged to accept that all selfishness, however slight and however legitimate it may appear at the time, can only lead to disaster. I did not study Antoine's needs as I should have. Looking back at my relationship with Father and the part I played in his life, I have to ask myself whether in submitting to his advances I was not unconsciously intent on keeping him to myself and preventing his remarriage. Even as a child – particularly, perhaps, as a child – I must have known that had he remarried he would have had less time to devote to me. How wise we become in retrospect! At the time, I was only conscious that I loved him and he loved me and from this love was born something of such significance that any other experience would be measured against it. We had a secret in which no one else would ever share. We were bound by this secret for all time. People used to remark how 'close' the Professor and his daughter were, how the Professor 'doted' on his only child. What a comfort she was to him since he lost his wife! All this was said with approbation. I do not believe anyone had the least suspicion that our relationship was intimate or I am sure Father would have heard mutterings. Father was above suspicion, respected as a scholar and, in the utterly materialistic atmosphere of Switzerland, approved of for being rich. It was not remarkable that I was indulged by him. It would have been remarkable had he not indulged me.

I was in my early twenties when I met Antoine. I had a degree in European History and a special interest in ancient cookery. I wrote a paper on the gastronomy of classical Greece for a French history review and was involved helping Father with his research into aphrodisiacs. Our work together was giving us great pleasure. Throughout my life until that time I had always experienced a powerful sense of well-being reading and writing in the safety of the oak-panelled library, among Father's collection of old cookery books, manuscripts and herbals. Father's archive was celebrated throughout the world; carefully maintained with humidifiers, behind half-lowered blinds, it smelt of beeswax, leather and Havana cigars. Being able to come and go amongst these treasures had made me feel special. At a very early age, Father would sit me down and show me the old illustrations of vegetables and herbs and tell me stories about meals in ancient times.

Observing the direction in which my interest appeared to be leading me, Father started to accompany me round Europe and North America to all the finest restaurants to observe how they were run, what food they served and in what surroundings. These journeys were useful not only from a practical point of view, but provided a glorious background to our intimacy. The sheer luxury in which we indulged our sensuality, combined with the passion I had developed for what

I had come to see as my subject for the rest of my life, made me feel I really had got everything I could possibly want.

When we learned that Father had cancer, I dealt with the possibility of its being fatal by denial. Yes, he had cancer, but... We flew at once to New York, to the leading prostate cancer specialist, and were reassured that with treatment the malignancy would be controlled. Professor Schwartz in New York detailed a consultant in Geneva to supervise Father's regime. It was debilitating. Our life abruptly changed from one devoted to pleasure to one ruled by the laws of survival. But at the time it hardly felt like that. We never felt desperate. Indeed, we never discussed the cancer as being terminal, we simply got on with obeying the timetable drawn up for its treatment. We carried on with our work, but our routine became punctuated by journeys to and from the hospital and Father's need to rest — something for which he had seemed in the past to have had no need at all.

It was by chance that we happened to be at home when the chef from the Palace Hotel came to return a book he had borrowed. M. Bouloux had been a regular visitor to the château on his days off. He used to enjoy a walk over the hills alone, but on this occasion he was accompanied by a young trainee whom he left at the front door to enjoy the view over the lake, rather than introduce him into the château. I think he felt it would be an imposition. However, Father did not want the young man to feel unwelcome and had insisted Bouloux bring him into the library. The young man was Reg Wilkes.

Reg was uneducated, a working-class Englishman from the north-east with absolutely nothing notable about him, or so it appeared on the face of things. However, it was not long before Father recognized an empty vessel clamouring to be replenished and, delighting in his authority, he decided to fulfil that task. And so it was that in his sickness my father found a young man – of whom he could not possibly feel jealous – to become his disciple, someone to mould to be of use to his daughter when he was no longer available. I see now how controlling he was. I was not aware of this at the time.

Bouloux confided to Father that Reg was the most gifted young chef he had ever come across and that given the right circumstances he was likely to become celebrated. It was, he said, extraordinary in an Englishman. He had both skill and taste. He was oddly withdrawn and had difficulty with French, lacked all education – he had no idea how cookery had evolved. What a challenge for Father! His library was to become Reg's university.

I believe I did not notice him that first day when Father invited Reg into the library. I was certainly present; my husband subsequently insisted I had been there, that I was reading and did not look up from my book. How remarkable it is that the defining moments in life can bypass consciousness. During the succeeding months, when Father took it upon himself to introduce Reg to the *history* of food and its preparation, I did not sense for a moment that the young Englishman was being groomed for me.

What struck me about Reg, as I got to know him a little, was his passion for cookery and his earnestness to learn the background to a career that had somehow chosen him. This passion was at odds with everything else about him. He was keen to succeed, his determination intensifying with the desire to repay Father for the interest Father was showing in him. He had never had anyone in his family to encourage him and he may well have started to relate to my father as the father he would have liked to have.

It is impossible, try as I have over the years, to remember just how it came about that Reg and I, with Father's encouragement, began to consider creating a restaurant together. Just as Father had entered my sexual life imperceptibly, he infiltrated my career decision without my registering the fact. He did everything with such subtlety that he never aroused resistance in me. It was only when I found myself married to Reg that I looked back and traced the route I had taken to such an unsatisfactory personal destination. By then Father was dying. My husband was proving a genius in the kitchen but altogether inadequate elsewhere; indeed he was exhibiting signs of severe instability.

When I read Antoine's description of me and our life together in *I is Another*, I am both furious and mortified. The wretched woman who put together Antoine's story clearly had an agenda of her own. Was she in love with my poor, deranged husband? Antoine was as incapable of the thoughts she ascribed to him as he was of writing them down. No doubt in his derangement he imagined all sorts of events arising from his terrors, but that does not mean the events took place. And if his story is a fabrication, why should his assessment of me be any less?

To give an example: he kept his impotence from his amanuensis. He implied that it was my own sexual *froideur* that was the cause of our sexual inaction, abstinence in fact. Certainly, within the context of his account it would have seemed probable that, added to my other failings, my rejection of him at an intimate level might well have accounted for his frustration and his frustration for his derangement. But none of this was the case. Although I have to admit that I was grateful not to have had to submit myself to Antoine's fumblings, and took care not to initiate him into any of the alternatives to full sexual congress, Antoine seemed to accept his experience of inaction as a perfectly acceptable preference. His fantasies were romantic and childish. His inner life was nourished on thoughts of a castle on a hill, a maiden with long, gold hair at a window in the tower, a dragon at the portcullis and the ways in which to become a hero in overcoming such obstacles to true love.

If Antoine truly believed I was the cause of his misery, would he have chosen to take with him into his incarceration a photograph of me and a silk scarf of mine? No, he needed to see me and to smell my scent for the rest of his life.

Antoine knew nothing about me other than that which had relevance to my running Les Coteaux – and not everything involved in that. His concerns were limited to the restaurant and what food I required him to prepare. For that reason, I had no intention of obliging Dr Auerbach with information about myself, independent of Antoine.

∞

For a while, my decision not to accommodate the doctor's thirst for detail paid off. He stopped contacting me. Then, one day, I found a message on my answering machine asking me to contact him urgently. I feared something untoward had happened. Usually, Dr Auerbach followed this up with a letter. Had there been an accident? Had Antoine been killed by a fellow patient or killed a patient himself? I felt anxious and slept badly that night. By ten o'clock next morning I had contacted the surgery and agreed to an appointment the same day.

In the past, Dr Auerbach had specifically required me not to write to Antoine, or expect to hear from him. If I wished to know how his treatment was progressing, how he was physically, I could contact Dr Auerbach himself. By isolating Antoine, his treatment could proceed unimpeded; his chain of thought would not be broken by filtering the past through the present. Dr Auerbach had asked me whether I intended to divorce Antoine. I said there was no point since I had no intention of remarrying. That was helpful, the doctor said. However, I noticed how thoughtful he became. Might I not change my mind in the future? Circumstances change. No, I assured him, I could not change my mind. How could

I be so sure? I did not reply verbally, merely shrugged my shoulders.

I was struck that the doctor did not keep me waiting. That was unusual. He quickly reassured me that Antoine was alive. However, something had arisen during his treatment that was proving a serious impediment. Antoine was levelling serious allegations against me and my father and his therapist felt insufficiently informed to separate his delusions from the facts. Could I assist?

Antoine had reported that my father and I had been lovers, and a child had been born from that liaison. He accused my father of having manipulated him into marriage with me to make it appear I had left Switzerland for a legitimate reason and not because, as my father feared, the police investigation was getting close to the facts. Antoine told his therapist that the child was confined to a convent in Ticino and one day, when she was older and had access to her papers, his allegations would be confirmed.

I remember how calmly Dr Auerbach reported this to me and how closely he studied my face while he spoke. I was in shock, acutely aware. Indeed it was as if my whole nervous system had risen to the occasion. Every muscle in my body harnessed itself into stasis, neither tightening nor relaxing to give expression to what I was thinking and feeling. Once Dr Auerbach had reported Antoine's allegations, he enlarged on their implications. I heard myself utter just one word: 'nonsense!' I noticed how gelid and controlled the word emerged, as if in splints. I got to my feet. Why was I leaving so soon, the doctor mocked? there was so much more he wished to tell me. *Tant pis!* I thought. There was nothing more I wished to hear. I moved towards the door. Dr Auerbach rushed forward to place himself between me and my escape. Something alien was taking hold of me. I remember a scalding sensation mount in my chest and neck. My face burnt. My hair stood on end. Automatically, my arm extended itself towards a small bronze sculpture, a horse and rider by Marini, which stood on a shelf. As if in slow motion I brought this exquisite work of art down on Dr Auerbach's head and then against his heart. For the lifetime of a few seconds I watched the quintessence of surprise and alarm overtaking him. Gradually, with his back resting against the door, he slipped to the floor. I had some difficulty pulling at his considerable weight to make my escape. I do not remember leaving the consulting room or getting out of the house. Evidently, I did so without the receptionist noticing. I flagged a passing taxi in Harley Street and gave as my destination my home address. Later, in Court, the driver gave evidence. He had noticed, he said, how peculiarly calm I had been for someone whose clothes were blood-soaked.

∞

And now I am confined at Riverside. Antoine has been released. His condition ameliorated from the day he brought his charges against me. Since he was no threat to anyone but me, and I was out of the way, his case was quickly reassessed. His behaviour here had been impeccable, as one might have expected. Not only had he volunteered to do all the cooking, he organized a superb vegetable garden. He is still spoken of with affection and admiration.

Once I was sentenced, I was put in a London hospital for the insane under observation. I believe I was sent up here to Riverside in a fit of bureaucratic exasperation. Authorities of any kind cannot abide those who offer neither explanation nor excuse for their actions. A solicitor and barrister were allotted to me but I chose not to instruct them. I let them plead as they saw fit. In the circumstances, that of my not speaking, they pleaded my insanity. Observing my silence, the Court accepted this diagnosis. And here, at Riverside, I have refused all psychotherapy. I prefer to be considered 'difficult' and 'uncooperative' than to reveal anything of that part of my life dearest to me. Of that I shall not be robbed. No doubt they keep me on here in the belief that one day I shall speak. I shall not.

It is unlikely I would be understood. In my heart I believe that Dr Auerbach deserved to die. He had no right to persist in trying to out my confidences. It has become a habit for people, be they doctors, journalists, spiritual advisers or even ordinary members of the public, to regard themselves entitled to every detail of another's thoughts and experiences. I do not share this view. I believe we have a right to challenge it at every opportunity. It is one thing for the intellectual to offer his insights voluntarily, for the artist to deliver his creations in return for a living, for men and women to tender their affections in mutual love, and proffer suggestions when asked for them, but it is unreasonable, immoral and distasteful to consume other people's lives without their consent and where there is no mutuality. I choose to remain mute.

Antoine has divorced me. I never did get the chance to ask him why he made accusations against me — and on what evidence. He was not to know what was true and what was false. Just emptying himself of suspicion may have proved his salvation. Did he know it would prove my damnation, my living death?

The Banana-Skin Tree

MANY HUNDREDS OF YEARS PAST, a shipload of men whose mission was to forsake the known world for the unknown, to live apart from civilization, stumbled on an island they thought might suit them. But because they found the island inhabited it was not paradise. They weighed anchor precipitously, having taken on provisions and ravaged the female population. It was the invaders who named the island 'Nabanas', intending an insult: only the bananas that grew in abundance were to be dignified, not the people.

Generations of islanders thereafter, whose understanding of time was limited to the passage between nightfall and day rise and the phases of the moon, were unable to testify as to when this invasion had taken place. However, fragments of the event emerged from the legends and rituals round which the community coalesced. And there was undeniable material evidence; some of the islanders were uncharacteristically light-skinned and had angular features.

None but those *en route* for paradise are likely to happen upon Nabanas. The island is remote, always seeming to fray the horizon. It is, of course, self-sustaining; an abiding, well-tempered climate facilitates crops to burgeon abundantly, abetted by husbandry that is second nature to the peasants who sow and reap, and herdsmen who tend sheep and goats for their milk, meat and hides. Around the shore the sea breathes deeply and easily, an ever-open invitation to the fishermen to cast their nets. However, despite such idyllic conditions, the islanders are imbued with traces of anxiety. The experience of invasion in their past has left remnants of unease; the exquisite balance and harmony of life on Nabanas cannot be taken for granted but must be diligently defended if it is not to fall victim to assault.

This intimation surfaced when in the recoverable past the banana crop started to dwindle. Few flower spikes ripened into hands of fruit and the few fingers that poked into life proved crooked and fleshless. Eventually the crop failed altogether.

The islanders gathered to confer. Although the opinions of each were of equal value, a few citizens had stood out from the crowd in the past by showing themselves unusually skilled in evaluating the consequences of actions they all agreed upon to take.

Amrit's foresight had attracted attention for being devoid of the slightest tincture of self-interest. He wondered out loud: was nature telling them something? They must listen and obey. It was useless to persist with the cultivation of anything doomed. They would concentrate their efforts on the olive and almond trees, the guavas, paw-paw and melons, all of which fruited without fuss.

Throughout the island the peasants uprooted their trees in the banana groves and used the fibrous debris for fuel.

In addition to his other unique qualities, Amrit the fisherman was a safeguarder, a man whose appreciation of the history that adhered to the most trifling of things — his knife, spoon and beaker, his fishing nets and wading boots — was keen. It was not, therefore, surprising that the sole banana tree that was to avoid destruction was his. He had cherished it throughout his life, not only for the fruit it once bore but for the memories it embodied. The tree had been the focal point of his ancestors' domestic life and now it was his. It was in its shade that he took his rest, chewed the fat with his wife Sudik and luxuriated in memory. The tree was a living member of his family. He asked nothing more of it than its continuing survival.

Amrit was mending his nets. Sudik was shelling peas.

Galvanized by their chores, their attention was unbroken by the deep breathing sea and the screeching gulls. The couple derived a special contentment being engrossed in their work in the company of the other.

His task completed, Amrit rose, threw his nets over his shoulder and prepared to make tracks for the harbour. Before setting out to rejoin his crew his custom was to touch the trunk of his tree with the two fingers he had first laid to his lips. While he was making this gesture of affection and respect, he was astonished to find what appeared to be pancake-flat bananas sprouting all over the bark of the tree. He let drop his nets and passed both his hands over the beautiful yellow fruit that seemed to be swelling to ripeness. But he quickly discovered the skins were not only flat but empty. His tree had no mind to bear fruit but thick, juicy husks. The bounty of the earth, the rain and the sun that had germinated sweet flesh in the past were now propagating nothing but the outward appearance of bananas. Amrit felt disturbed and, believing it would be harmful to the tree to leave waste to decay on it, he picked the useless crop and left it in a pile in the lane. He estimated such rubbish would rot in the sun within days, and make good fertilizer.

∞

It is late afternoon. Amrit and his crew have prepared the boat and gathered at the harbour café. Every day they sit here waiting for the sun to sink before lighting the oil lamps by which they will fish. Sometimes they talk, sometimes they sing. This afternoon they are drinking palm wine and playing dominoes. Each is agonizing behind a little wall of counters erected before him, counters he has chiselled from the bones of goats and incised with lines and pips. Each man – and there are eight of them at play – concentrates deeply, creating an impenetrable stillness at the heart of bustling café activity. But Amrit has been gripped by a sense of unease and feels menaced. His mind is untidy with thoughts of his banana-skin harvest rotting in the lane. It is only with a supreme effort of will that he can tidy those thoughts away and drag his attention back to his counters. He bangs one down and is immediately challenged by his neighbour who hurls one of his own alongside and then his neighbour's neighbour who takes up the challenge and the game gathers momentum and hurtles to an end. 'Enough!' Amrit cries. Accounts are settled. The men rise, push back their chairs and join friends at the bar for a final draught before bidding the land-locked villagers goodnight.

When Amrit turns his back on the café and feels the door swing closed, the sense of being watched burns his back. Pursued by menace, he feels his scalp tighten and his whole body fill with an agitation that makes him shudder. He hurries to place himself shoulder to shoulder within the shelter of the group with whom he will shortly be putting to sea. This solidarity is not, however, as reassuring as it should be. He is haunted by the thought that it is unwise to set sail threatened by the unknown.

The wicks are cut and clean, the lamps burn bright. The wind is gentle and the sea flat. There is a full moon and nothing in the air on the tin-plate water to aggravate Amrit's feelings of dread. Yet, he reflects, for the first time in his life he is aware that there is something unnatural about working nights. Surely, the setting of the sun is a signal for man and beast to stretch out and, having sown their seed, practise for the longest sleep of all?

The catch is as abundant as ever and the boat returns safely to harbour. But when Amrit releases the haul from the nets, and the fish lie strewn on the deck, he finds himself having to sort benign, good-eating subjects from venomous sting-fish, weavers and leech-rays, fish with concealed glands on their dorsal fins, fish that emit poison from their spines and inflict painful wounds, whose tails are coated in fungus that can eat into human flesh. Never before has Amrit had to deal with these beasts. He grew up knowing that such exist and could pose a danger but has never before had to face them. He kept the matter from his mate.

On his way home, Amrit stops in the lane and examines the pile of banana skins. The sun has robbed them of their colour and returned them a musty smell. Amrit feels tired and tormented. He wanders into the yard in front of his cottage and peers up at his tree through half-closed eyes. Can it really be that more skins are sprouting? This would be appalling, an aberration of nature.

Amrit is a man of habit. He has lived his life in a world without surprises. Every morning, returning from a night at sea, his routine has been unchanging: a meal and six hours' sleep. His wife is accustomed to a husband of equable nature and this is lacking today. Amrit has scraped his chair loudly against the floor before sitting down at table. He has banged his spoon against his bowl with every mouthful. He has snapped at her and abandoned his meal before finishing the good things she set before him. And now she hears him stamping upstairs and positively throwing himself down on the bed.

He sleeps fitfully. He wakes tired and preoccupied. By the time he has gathered his forces and rejoined his crew, the café is crowded. Not only is he later than usual, he will drink more than usual. Whereas all about him – the conversation, the dominoes, the laughter and the ringing of the till – appears the same as usual, Amrit senses something changed. What confronts him may look familiar on the surface but what is happening beneath the surface is strange. To steady himself he takes stock. He counts the stone jars in which the palm wine ferments; he counts the beakers from which it is served. He ticks off the fruit in the earthenware bowls, the nuts in the baskets, the sliced and pickled vegetables in the jars. He watches while the loaves of bread are first divided and then apportioned. He must memorize every detail before they dissolve. Men are exchanging information. He cannot hear what intricacies are under discussion but notices the calm consideration they are lent. There is no contention. All is cooperation, encouragement and affection. Amrit closes his eyes and reconstitutes the reassuring scene in his mind and holds it there. He holds it for as long as its outlines retain their shape, and then he opens his eyes and brings both hands down on the bar and clutches it. It feels substantial. But is it? Are six men playing dominoes? Are four of the elders smoking clay pipes in the corner?

The door to the café is opening. A stranger stands at the threshold. He is dressed in black: suit, shoes and wide-brimmed hat. He is surveying the scene. No one but Amrit notices him. Amrit wants to ask someone whether he knows who this is but everyone is occupied in conversation and he is loath to interrupt. He finds himself ordering another drink. He is not drunk, he is certain of that. He always avoids the drink that would bring him to an altered state of mind. What he wants from a drink is the sweet reinforcement of determination the one before the final drink ensures. Yet things do seem to be slipping out of control. First his banana tree: should he not have felled his like everyone else felled theirs? What would his neighbours say if they knew that he alone, against the decision they had come to as a community, had preserved his? They would certainly laugh to see his crop of husks. They would no doubt say it served him right and did he not have enough to do with his time without having to peel husks from the tree for the rest of his life? Then there was nature's second miscreation: the venomous fish he netted, fish with treacherous weapons of assault primed to strike. Normally, these varieties steer clear of the nets. What could be the message from that encounter? He knew he and his crew had been in real danger and, furthermore, the beasts might have turned on the good catch and rendered them uneatable. Amrit felt himself netted in distress.

And now the stranger is at his side. He has moved imperceptibly from the door, through the crowd. He is asking Amrit what he is drinking and when Amrit tells him orders two beakers of palm wine from the bar. He has called Amrit by name. He says he has observed the fisherman piling banana skins in the lane. Amrit feels threatened: he is doing something he should not be doing and has been found out. Who is this man? How does he know my name and where I live and what I do? Amrit takes a while to answer the stranger's questions, which are coming one after the other on a tide of interrogation. Eventually he finds his voice and tells the man he is using the useless crop to make fertilizer for his vegetable patch. Sure, the stranger retorts, the ground on Nabanas is so fertile that that is not required? Amrit quickly answers that he cannot stand waste. This answer is clearly one with which the stranger can identify and he tells Amrit that he is just the same: cannot abide waste. Indeed, that is precisely why he has come to see Amrit, to negotiate the *purchase* of this crop. Amrit is stunned! He throws back his head and swallows the drink he knows he should not have accepted. The stranger's voice is not a loud one and yet Amrit can hear every word he utters above the noise of the cafe. He says he is of the opinion that Amrit's tree will produce a continuous crop of banana skins, and for his purposes this is an essential requirement for he needs the material in perpetuity. What makes this man imagine I would *sell* my crop? I don't need money. I have enough. Enough!

The word 'enough' echoed in Amrit's head. If there was one thing that separated Amrit from the stranger it was that Amrit epitomized 'enough' and the stranger 'excess'. The stranger was wearing too many clothes, quite unsuitable for Nabanas. He had gold bits and pieces at his neck and wrist. His manner was too sure. He drank too much. Amrit did not like being too anything: too hot, too full, too tired – even too happy.

Anyone with a use for the skins had only to say and he would be delighted to *give* them away. He was only harvesting the husks to protect his tree from the rot they would encourage if left on the bark. He only preserved them for fertilizer because he could not abide waste, and there was nothing else they were any good for. For what did the stranger want them?

Amrit's thoughts circled in his head and fastened on their own tails. The next time he looked towards the stranger he found him gone. As suddenly as he had happened at Amrit's side, he had disappeared.

Instead of allowing his thoughts to confuse him, he should have asked the stranger to tell him for what precisely he wanted the skins. But if he had shown curiosity it would have encouraged the man to think his offer to buy was tempting.

Amrit had never felt desire for anything beyond what he had but, he reflected, he had never been in a position to acquire more. The fishing was good enough to create the surplus necessary to barter for other food, and the wherewithal to keep his house and boat in a good state of repair. He paid the medicine man in fish, and the school his children attended with hours narrating sea-salted legends. The economy of Nabanas was uncomplicated; everyone contributed what he had and took what he needed. The system worked equally well for all. There was always enough.

In the weeks following Amrit's encounter with the stranger he went to sea and returned home safely, but without peace of mind. He peeled the skins from his tree and saw the pile grow to reach the top of the wall separating his cottage from the lane. His anxiety was tidal but did not withdraw completely when he managed to sleep. In his dreams he found himself suspended over chasms, held high on giant waves above a boiling sea and subject to all the trials of Tantalus. Should he not have felled his tree like everyone else felled theirs? On the one hand, yes. On the other, was there not a case for acknowledging that the tree's function was greater than that of usefulness? And to preserve the husks for the vegetable patch was much in keeping with the lore of the land. But the crop was starting to emit a foul stench and Sudik was complaining. She told Amrit to cart the whole pile down to the sea and dump it before the flies got to it. The idea did not appeal to Amrit, who thought the crabs and mussels might suffer from the noxious effluent.

In the fullness of time, the stranger reappeared. Amrit was returning home after a night's fishing and saw from a distance a man on his knees in the lane, picking through a pile of banana skins, as if to test them for some quality or other. As he approached nearer, the man straightened himself and, brushing one hand against the other, attempted to wipe away the slipperiness. He greeted Amrit warmly. He said he had come that day because he felt in his bones that Amrit was readying himself to talk to him. Somewhat disconcerted by the stranger's apparent clairvoyance, Amrit nevertheless refrained from asking him to explain his supernatural powers. Instead, he listened to the stranger outline his intentions. He would remove the skins from the lane at every full moon and in return leave whatever Amrit ordered for himself and his family. He could supply silks for Sudik, nets and oars for Amrit, toys for the children, potions to assure longevity for the whole family, that sort of thing. Did Amrit have any questions?

'Just one, for now,' Amrit replied. 'Where do you come from?'

'Elsewhere,' the stranger said.

And he disappeared.

Amrit would have been almost perfectly happy if the stranger had not reappeared. He sensed that curiosity was the gate to temptation. He was very curious to know for what purpose the stranger wanted the banana skins. When the stranger did reappear, unexpectedly soon, Amrit asked him what had prompted his return. The stranger laughed. 'I have an uncanny way of knowing when the time is ripe.' Amrit felt uncomfortable and quickly interrupted the guffaws by saying he would need to know for what purpose the banana skins were intended; they had lost their colour, they had become tough on the outside and slimy on the inside, they had a musty smell.

The stranger brushed aside these details. He was in the entertainment business, he explained. Entertainment? What was that? Amrit was to learn that on Elsewhere there existed a distinction between that which was work and that which was leisure. Work was onerous, leisure was fun. Indeed, in order to get people on Elsewhere to work at all, those in power (power?) had to design both times and locations for fun at which their people were provided with divertissement. The best fun, that is to say the fun that most people enjoyed, took the form of discomforting the poor, the weak and the disabled. The stranger explained that they were the butt because they were useless for the 'Advancement of Elsewhere'.

By now Amrit was well out of his depth. 'Advancement' had meaning for him only in the sense of motion, of going forward in his boat. The idea of the island of Nabanas advancing was quite terrifying; he did not so much as wish to imagine the island moving under its own or any other steam. As for the poor, there were none on Nabanas. The concept was understood and distribution made to overcome such an eventuality. So far as those weaker than others were concerned, on Nabanas they simply did the lighter work. As for the disabled, if someone had an accident it was regarded as a privilege to give him special protection. The stranger's explanations were disorientating and rather than stand giddy in the lane, Amrit invited the stranger into the yard and sat down with him under the tree. 'Tell me more about Elsewhere!' he suggested. The stranger felt encouraged. At once he told of the inexhaustible, unstinting wealth and comfort in his land. Amrit was shocked; the description of opulence made his head ache and stomach churn. The stranger finished his account by weighing the plenitude on Elsewhere against the want on Nabanas. Amrit did not understand that the calculation was intended to reflect badly on Nabanas.

Amrit told the stranger emphatically that he would on no account sell or ever give him the banana skins. Firstly, he had no need of anything over and above that which his fishing provided. Second, he was not going to contribute to the fun of the people on Elsewhere whose enjoyment depended upon seeing their fellows brought low. On Nabanas, he said, the happiness of one led to the happiness of all. The stranger muttered 'sentimental' under his breath. He rose from his seat and cursed the day he set sail for Nabanas. It had been a waste of time and money, Elsewhere's two most precious commodities. If now that banana skins were unobtainable he was going to have to come up with some new idea 'to amuse the folks back home'.

Amrit watched the stranger slouch off. Somehow he knew the man would not return.

Times had been unsettling. Things had veered off course. He must untangle his thoughts and settle his mind. It seemed to Amrit that the unease he had recently felt and the peculiar experiences he had endured had much to do with his having taken it upon himself to act independently of the community. He had agreed with one and all on an action he himself had failed to take. He had not even discussed whether he had a case for acting differently. He had got above himself. He had allowed himself to believe in the assessment of himself the community had made: that the skill he had for evaluating the consequence of action somehow set him apart from the majority. Of course, he was no better at forecasting than anyone else on the island. Perhaps their readiness to accord him status was due to their desire to avoid taking responsibilities.

Amrit's tree continued to produce a crop of waste. The pile in the lane grew higher and wider. At last Amrit realized he had to do something, for the smell in the lane was fetid. He made a start. He shovelled a few buckets of skins into the yard and made a bonfire. He stood back and watched the skins shrivel to a dry dust. Peculiarly, they did not create heat but gave off a fragrant, intoxicating scent.

Amrit was astonished to experience the transformation of the fetid to the fragrant and saw it as a sign, and was reassured. Neighbours were attracted to his yard and chose to sit with him under the tree. Little by little the yard which provided sanctuary for the sole surviving banana tree became a hallowed meeting place for the islanders, a place in which to gather where the history of Nabanas was most keenly felt.

Work

'DON'T ASK ME ABOUT WORK! Don't so much as mention the word! I'm not going to do any. I've told Gertie not to look for any and not to accept anything. I'm finished with work!'

I felt put in my place. I should not have enquired. But I also felt sad for Jess. I was sure that part of her longed to get back into the business. We had been having one of our long Sunday afternoon telephone conversations and it was characteristic of Jess to round it off with a proclamation.

Control answered her demons; Jess went to every effort to assert dominance over her environment, and authority over others. Her days followed a formula. She repeated the events of yesterday and planned tomorrow to resemble today. She left no room for an exceptional event, she neither looked forward to such nor would she know how to deal with it. And because she did not know how to be alone, she had certain difficulties coping with being with others, and needed to plan her outings with friends to strict limits. 'We'll meet at Pâtisserie Valérie at eleven. Should you get there before me, don't forget: I have to sit in the smoking area. We'll trot round Harrods after coffee. Oh, I'll need to make a detour into Beauchamp Place for my specs . . . No, I shall certainly not accompany you to a cinema. You know I don't like to sit in a confined place with strangers. Anyhow, I'll need a shut-eye. I've got my accountant coming to supper. Not a lot of fun. I'll take him over the road to the little French restaurant . . .' Jess never cooked a meal. It would have messed up her kitchen.

She and I went back a long way. We had become best friends at school when we were thirteen. Even then I was dazzled by a quality she had to which I could not then give a name. Later I was to recognize it as glamour. Jess had a way of walking, of holding her head high on her long, straight neck, her chin tucked in, peering over the heads of her contemporaries. Her school uniform was always immaculately clean and its pleats knife-edged. She was quiet and unobtrusive in class and so markedly courteous that I noticed teachers doing a double-take when she spoke, as if they were wondering whether there were not a trace of irony in Jess's tone.

Jess quickly assigned to me the role of her fixer. This had its initiation in the classroom where I supplied her with the solutions to problems she could not solve, led to the gym where I fabricated excuses for her absences and, ultimately, to the larder from which I stole fruit, nuts and raisins to subdue her hunger. Jess could not, would not eat the concoctions masquerading as food served to girls at boarding school all over the country during World War II. She was resolved in her determination not to endure any sport and to this end arranged for doctors' letters to support her claim to back trouble. Nor did she allow herself to be corralled into the school play or poetry readings. I did not understand this at the time. Only later did I realize that from an early age Jess was preparing herself for a professional life she kept from her family and from me.

When I left school for university Jess, against all expectation and family ruckus, applied to RADA. We lost touch – a matter more of geography than anything else. Inevitably, however, we made new friends. Then we both married unwisely, she to a homosexual actor and I to an alcoholic doctor. At this time we tracked each other down and in a spirit of disillusion propped one another up for a bit. I gathered my forces and went abroad to do postgraduate work, Jess joined a rep company and went to the west country. She needed the money but it was exiguous and it came as a huge relief to her when she was 'discovered' in a scant bathing costume on a rocky beach and whisked to Hollywood and a batch of forgettable 'B' movies.

Over the years I would check the telephone directory for Jess's entry. I was forced to conclude she was either out of the country or ex-directory and I rather forgot her. Then I read in the *Evening Standard* that she had been in the States for years and was now back in England for good. '"It's home and I missed it!" Jess Johnson told our reporter, prior to her departure for Bolton where she is to play Miss Croft in *Ghosts in Mourning*.' I don't know why I did not get in touch now that I knew she was back in the country and for good. Maybe I feared that our occupations would divide us, that a childhood friendship was not basis enough for lives which had become so different from each other.

Astonishingly, it was not until we were in our early sixties that we got together again, and that was by chance. We met at a bus stop opposite Harrods. Instant recognition: we gasped, embraced and without noticing its number, rode a bus to the terminus catching up on thirty years of ups and downs. From that blessed encounter we fell into a routine of speaking on the telephone every Sunday and meeting once every couple of weeks to talk over coffee (Jess seemed almost never to eat), and shop.

The average woman does not look forward to her sixties and once they have crept up and consumed her they only confirm her worst expectations. For having emerged from the fifties with her femininity pretty well intact, she now finds it dissolved into thin air. She is invisible. Gone from sight.

Men and women bump into her in the street and allow swing doors to catch her in the face. Shop assistants do not assist. It is not as if she were old, she tells herself, not as if she were seventy, heaven forfend! If she were in her seventies, at least she would not be expected to stand in the bus while the school children sat eating their crisps and drinking their Cokes. In her sixties the English woman is still a work-horse and more than that because she is retired, she 'has the time'. No good can come of having 'time on your hands', only depression. At every turn she is advised to 'keep busy', attend the University of the Third Age, serve in a charity shop, take up painting/violin/bonsai . . . spend the winters on the Costa del Sol, keeping the hotels open. Such admonitions, cheerfully and freely distributed, are not issued with sympathy for dropped arches suddenly collapsed under the weight of her comfort-eating, nor with the problems she has finding clothes for an age group disregarded by designers who either assume she is not interested in fashion or simply hope she is no more. No one wants to know that coffee keeps her awake through the night and rich food gives her acid indigestion, that her bladder interrupts her enjoyment of theatres and concerts and that stress of the merest sort brings on migraine. No, that sympathy is reserved for her *old* age, when the sheltered housing will cope. She has merely reached the bus pass stage and is very lucky to be the recipient of it and her old-age pension.

Jess, however, was largely free from the victimizations imposed by society on the retired. She did not permit her body to fall prey to disease. She chain-smoked not because she was addicted but because she enjoyed it. She seemed to prove new scientific evidence that pleasure activates the immune system. She had exceptionally good looks, plenty of money and belonged to a glamorous profession. Her refusal to be dictated to by others resulted in a strikingly even temper. She did not allow anyone or anything to make her raise her voice – or lower it. She laughed, but not excessively. She never whined but referred lightly and with humour to those aspects of modern living that did not quite come up to her expectations. Her *aperçus* reminded me that she was an unreconstructed child of pre-World War II, from a rather pinched, uneducated background.

She had all the money she required for a lifestyle with which she was thoroughly satisfied. She had earned and saved and had insurance policies that matured in her sixties. She was mystified as to why not everyone had managed their financial affairs similarly. There was no room in her calculations for even the 'deserving' poor. Her complacency often irritated me severely and I would feel hostile, but she would quickly redeem herself by innocently proclaiming that she loved life because she had such excellent women friends.

'The last thing I need is a man!' she said in response to my suggestion that she might consider remarrying. 'Nothing but trouble, men, except for the odd little elderly queer and I have a couple of those on the back burner to call upon in desperate circumstances. They are indispensable, you know, for choosing paint colours and flowers. Now that's one thing in my single status I just can't face: buying flowers for myself. I know the flat often cries out for fresh flowers but I'm too used to having them bought for me.'

One Sunday Jess devoted her call to a description of her recent experiences in the ante-room to the haematology department of her local NHS hospital, where she had had to wait hours without benefit of *The Field* or *Tatler*. 'They're a different species from us, don't you agree?' she observed of her fellow-patients. Without waiting for me to support her, she continued, 'I couldn't even understand what they were talking about. Probably rather a good thing. I doubt they have much of interest to communicate. And they speak such an odd variant of English. Every second word is fuck. And have you noticed how they have completely disposed of the letter "t" and how they repeat "basically" and "yer know what I mean" at the start and finish of every sentence? You'd never say "basically" would you? Promise? They don't seem hygienic. I was quite nervous of germs.' Jess elaborated yet more outrageously, giving me time to work out if and when I might – without showing the exasperation I felt – point out that poverty leading to poor health and exclusion leading to poor articulation were more likely causes of the differences she had observed than the existence of Martian genes.

Following such a conversation, I used to wonder why I put up with Jess's prejudices when I didn't with those of anyone else. I discussed this lack of consistency with my friend Yvonne who noted that nevertheless I always spoke of Jess with particular affection and found myself able to laugh at the worst of her opinions. 'At our age we can't afford to fall out with everyone who doesn't share our views,' Yvonne observed.

Given that Jess had so recently forbidden me to use the word 'work' in her presence, it came as a surprise when she rang to say that she had agreed to do an unveiling and give a little chat of appreciation in front of a group of theatre folk. 'They're erecting a plaque to Frieland Jarvis.'

'Who he?'

'A director I worked with years ago. Loved my work! Was forever on about my gift for comedy. I've been told how flattered he would be to know I was pulling the string in his honour. It's being organized by the Mayor of Bayswater. Frieland lived close to me in Moscow Road.' I rather wondered what had persuaded Jess to do this because to her, I knew, it constituted 'work'. However, it was a solo performance and she would have no lines to commit to memory. 'I shall get Archie to lend me his arm,' she added. I understood. Archie was one of her paint and floral experts.

When next Jess rang she reported that there had been quite a crowd in Moscow Road and several old chums had met the same evening for dinner at the Royal China. She spoke enthusiastically about actors – male and female – she had not seen or spoken to for years. Trotting briskly down memory lane, she remembered plays she had appeared in and with whom, dingy digs she had lodged in and with whom, and ghastly meals they had eaten together. I felt something in her was giving, responding to the adrenalin this encounter – and the memories it aroused – had provoked.

Jess adored her home, a large flat lacquered with the gloss of latter-day success, overlooking Hyde Park. She couldn't bear to be away from it for more than a few hours. It was as if she needed to check it was still where she had left it, in the shiny state in which she kept it. She had had it decorated white throughout. White walls, white carpet, white covers on outsize sofas and easy chairs and white curtains at the huge windows. She had even found white television sets and white frames for her pictures – mostly photographs and theatre posters. In each of the four rooms one wall was mirror glass. The only colour in that flat was Jess herself reflected.

'I love my life!' she reminded me again when I was visiting her. 'It's this flat. I can't get back to it quickly enough when I've been in town. It's my haven. I don't want posh dinners and grand parties at the end of the day. I'd never take a cruise. I just want home, alone, wrapped in my candlewick dressing gown, in front of the box.' My reaction was one of shock that Jess wrapped herself in candlewick. I would have imagined her draped in satin. She went on to describe her nightly hair and skin routine and the exhausting Swedish exercises she always did.

I found something oddly contradictory between the appearance Jess presented to the world and her stylish environment and her complete lack of social life: no dinners, no theatres, certainly no charity balls, no weekends in Paris, no Caribbean cruises ... But she was the only actress I knew and I wondered whether I did not have a false idea of the universal glamour of their lives. Jess frequently repeated that what was important to her were the friends she saw during daylight hours, all of whom were women. She seemed to have one for each of life's necessities, rather in the manner of an outfit for each of the half-dozen occasions that arose. She rarely referred to her friends by their names but by the names she had given them. I was her 'brainy' friend. She had a 'caring' friend, a 'needy' friend and an 'arty' friend. There were others. She kept us apart from one another, but always in my presence spoke kindly and appreciatively of everyone.

I was her 'brainy' friend only, I think, because she saw me as the one person she knew who read thick books with small print sometimes in a language she did not recognize. She never asked me what I was doing professionally. Our conversations revolved around what she wanted to buy, what plans she had for her body, a certain amount of harmless gossip about one or other of her friends – and memories of our shared past. I remember her laying before me her *modus vivendi*: 'I can only do one thing at a time. I've got to settle the matter of the lampshades. Once I've got them sorted out I can think about some winter clothes. And then, once my cupboards are full, I can get the flat feng shui'd. Then – and only then – I shall ring the wonderful Dr X and make an appointment to organize a little tuck.' Jess was so outstandingly beautiful, the idea of her even considering plastic surgery was preposterous and we almost came to blows over the subject. But I was nearing an understanding that Jess had so little with which to occupy herself she needed to think up possibilities for a future to give herself something passing for purpose. Having decided not to work, what was there but lampshades, winter clothes and a 'little tuck'?

She was complaining of her failing memory, but when I said I had the same problem and had to write down everything – and produced a notebook from my bag to prove it –

she waved her hand in a gesture of dismissal. I think had she found a crocodile-skin notebook she might have been persuaded to use it, but my own example certainly did nothing to inspire her. I suggested going to see a play in which Maggie Smith was giving a virtuoso performance. I told Jess I had two seats for a matinée. 'I couldn't,' she said. 'It would make me unbearably nervous', and she stressed 'unbearably'. 'I would be on tenterhooks throughout, worrying that darling Maggie would corpse. No, I just can't.'

On reflection I would say that my role in Jess's life was to listen. She certainly did not want me to express an opinion about her life. Perhaps I should have insisted, been more interventionist and interpreted what appeared to be so trivial. But I let it all slip down and never disturbed the sediment.

She had a more active life with her 'arty' friend from the theatre. With her she scoured the antique markets for the *bibelots* in onyx, silver, amber and tortoiseshell she strewed across her glass and chrome tables. With her 'needy' friend Susie, Jess exercised her charitable feelings and willingly accompanied her friend out to Ealing and Balham to visit unqualified practitioners of alternative medicine, mediums and fortune-tellers. I don't know what Jess got from these encounters. She did not tell me and I never asked. She used to go with her 'funny' friend Amy, the novelist, to readings at Waterstone's, but I never heard her say she had bought a book as a result. I know that she read Amy's books, given to her by Amy. She expressed abundant admiration for these rather literary novels, but no understanding. For her common experience was reality. On the single occasion Amy and I bumped into each other in Jess's flat, I watched the novelist elegantly skirt round the vexed questions Jess posed as to the identity of her characters. The fact that in one novel Amy's narrator was a girl child and in the next an adult male confused Jess, who not only could not grasp that the narrator may not double for the author but believed that every novel was an autobiography. Amy was far too polite — and fond of Jess — to explain. Jess had the effect on us all, I think, of making us behave rather more considerately in her presence than elsewhere. Whatever her inadequacies, nothing took away from her friends a sense of gratitude towards her for her friendship, rather as one is grateful to the sun if it deigns to shine.

'Gertie rang. They want me in Rome next month!' This information issued one weekday afternoon arrived barked down the wires rather as if it were news of an assassination. I was taken off-guard, didn't know how to respond. I decided on a neutral tone for 'Sounds attractive!' There was a pause and I added, 'Better than Rotherham!'

'Very good outfit,' Jess said with satisfaction.

'What to do?' I asked.

'Biscuit ad.'

'Well, could have been worse. Could have been incontinence pads.'

'I have to wear hunting gear and speak Spanish on a horse. Must go now. Bye!'

Occasionally, when she was being particularly self-absorbed, Jess had a tendency to ignore questions posed and answer those she would rather have had put to her. This produced astonishing *non sequitur*s which I always promised myself I would make a note of — and never did. When I look back, I am forced to wonder whether her gift for *not* engaging was something she practised with her agent Gertie. Forty-eight hours after the biscuit ad call I received another.

'I'm not doing it!' No opening remark, no indication as to what she was referring, but straight *in medias res*, as if we had been speaking five minutes ago and I would have nothing else on my mind.

'Why?'

'Don't want to drag all that way.'

'Jess darling, I don't imagine they will be expecting you to foot it to Rome. You'll have first-class travel, a lovely hotel, delicious eats and drinks. And just think of the shopping!'

'There wouldn't be time. And you know I don't like abroad. Alone.'

'Take Susie!'

'No, it wouldn't work!'

'So, what've you told Gertie?'

'Nothing yet. But I will. I'll say the money's not right.'

'How much are they offering?'

'Two thousand, the Excelsior, limousines to and from the airports and no doubt all the cocktail biscuits I could eat in a lifetime. All for forty-eight hours away from my gorgeous flat. No, I just won't do it.'

'My God! I'd do just about anything for a thousand pounds a day.'

'No you wouldn't. You don't do anything for money!'

That reminded me. Jess had had a minor operation some months previously. When she was discharged from the London Clinic, I offered to do her supermarket shopping because she was advised not to lift loads for a while. I delivered enough food for a long seige and under her close surveillance stacked it away in her cupboards, fridge and freezer. She was obsessional; there was only one place for each item and I knew that if I put anything in the wrong place she would be up all night reorganizing. When she asked me for the bill she took out her cheque book and said she was going to add something to the total for my petrol and my time. I all but exploded.

'Jess, I'm your friend, your oldest friend, how on earth can you be offering to pay me?'

'Because you haven't got much.'

'Dear Jess, thanks but no thanks.'

'If I'd got someone from the agency I would have had to pay them.'

'Well, isn't it a good thing you've got friends!' How could she have imagined she was expected to make such a gesture? How could she have made such a *faux pas*? I didn't say that I appreciated the thought because I hadn't. Only much later when I went over this exchange did I wonder whether Jess was used to being scrounged off, or whether something in her make-up could not allow for the idea that anyone could take pleasure in doing things for her. I remembered that following this incident she got Susie to do the shopping, Susie who needed money but whose circumstances were such that she certainly did not need the extra work this little service involved.

There is no question but that Jess was appreciative of her women friends. We were her life's blood, but I doubt she loved any one of us. The friendship she and I enjoyed was cemented with our involvement with one another in childhood – something neither of us shared with anyone else. Neither her parents nor mine had wanted children and both sets had used the exigencies of wartime to farm us out. Our unsatisfactory marriages had been scuppered by a too keen need we recognized in one another. But when we got together in our sixties we had little else in common. I doubt we could have spent a holiday together successfully. We dared not discuss current events or social issues. We were Right and Left apart. Jess read the tabloids and magazines devoted to health and fashion. Not my staples. She haunted the Easy Listening basement at HMV. Not my bag. We took our recreation differently. Anyhow, from what did Jess need to rest? Resting?

She used to spend two weeks (the same two weeks) every year at a particular health farm. I never understood quite what she hoped to gain from the place. She had no need to lose weight. Her need was to lose anxiety – a matter not addressed by Tillingbury. Throughout her fourteen days there she never stopped to chain-smoke but she did hone exceptional diversionary skills to succeed in fooling the staff, and she regaled me with these on her return. Nor did she cease to pop her pills, the uppers and downers her Harley Street psychiatrist prescribed at regular three-monthly consultations, at the cost of £150 an hour. I gathered that notwithstanding the facials, massage, mud baths, manicures and pedicures, what Jess most enjoyed was the opportunity of getting together with a certain raddled tabloid journalist she much admired. Here was a woman who actually made a living from defining Members of Parliament and other public figures by their sexual preference and/or racial origin. Jess never expressed her prejudices to me. She dropped hints, but finding them fall on stony ground she knew to desist. Instead she put all the homophobia and racist remarks she found amusing in the mouth of the journalist. That way she could voice her own intolerances and I could freely criticize them.

Jess showed no taste for introspection. I always felt that to give her pills for depression was a cop-out and her psychiatrist should have sent her for therapy. But maybe he felt that she was never likely to modify her ingrained reactions because she did not dare examine the territory on which she had formed them. They were part of her background. She had been so pleased to leave that behind it never occurred to her that unless she purged herself of its influence, what was latent would always emerge. She did not understand the love resonances of the love-hate relationship.

∞

'Gertie rang. She wants me to get new photographs taken and she insists her man do them. It's going to cost me a bomb.' I knew it would upset her to be asked why Gertie wanted new photographs and why, given that it had to be something to do with work. In the event, Jess spent weeks preparing herself for the session, growing her hair to the length she preferred, trying out colours to dye it. She had gone grey years before but no one ever knew it. She had been every colour from ash-blond to cinnabar since.

She was haunting theatrical make-up places, experimenting with eye shadows and lipsticks in every shade from neutral through ginger to carmine. While she tried them in front of me, asking me what I thought, she spoke about parts for older actresses and how although it would be easier to let her hair go grey, put on a bit of weight even and throw out the make-up and accept character roles, she wasn't going to have any of it. She was going to stay firmly put in the glamour field and get the sorts of parts Coral Brown would be glad to accept. Despite the activity – and it was rather frenzied – I felt that preparing for a photo session had become an end in itself: that she had no further objective in mind.

We met for coffee at the Waldorf Hotel, a setting chosen by Jess for being comfortable and *passé* and having no smoking embargo. It was close to her preferred cosmetics supplier and on a direct bus route from her flat. We spent the morning talking round the subject of what work she would prefer to do were it not for the fact that she was never going to work again. It would have to be television. She had enjoyed her television parts and what with her faltering memory and her need to sleep normal hours and hating having to be on location miles away from home, a nice sit-com shot in the suburbs would be her choice. Anyhow, she loathed live theatre and was not going to put herself through a provincial tour, however much they paid her and it wouldn't be much anyhow. No, not at her time of life. Did I have any idea what theatrical digs could be like? Those curled sandwiches after the show? How icy the climate north of Watford? Never again!

I listened attentively. In my own life I had learned never

to say never. Why was Jess rehearsing this same subject? Was it because the lamp shades were *in situ*, the winter coat bought and the 'tuck' booked? Why had the to-work-or-not-to-work question become the most pressing in her repertoire? Should I prop her up in her expressed desire not to work, or in her unexpressed desire to get back on the boards?

Since I was always absorbed in my own work, I started to consider whether Jess observed that I was not suffering the identity problem undermining her. For who did she feel she was if she was not even making herself available for work? She had been an actress since she was fifteen – forty-three years – even if 'resting' had been playing an all-too-prominent role in her drama these past six or seven years.

She got out her cuttings book. Poring over very good notices and lovely photographs of Jess in undistinguished plays, I was able to 'ooh' and 'ahh' with genuine conviction. 'What a pity not to continue to do something you are so good at. You've had a lot of admiration and praise. You often enjoyed yourself...' I tried. 'Yes,' she murmured, as if trying an unfamiliar fruit for the first time and needing to be cautious before swallowing. 'I've been depressed, you know.' And then I raised the chicken/egg equation. Had she been depressed because she was not working or not working because she was depressed?

'Let's go across the road and have tea in that nice little café!'

∞

'Gertie rang.'

'Did she like the photos?'

'Very much.' Pause. Time enough for me to ponder 'timing'.

'There's a play they want me for.'

'How d'you feel about that?' I have heard psychotherapists use this tone.

'It's a whodunit.'

'Is that what you *want* to do?' Another pause, longer this time.

'I'd be good for the part. Anyhow, I've not been on the stage for eight years. I can't be too choosy. It's work after all.'

'But you don't want work. Or that's what I understood. You certainly don't *need* work. You're sixty-eight, you've got money in the bank and, forgive me for saying so, it's hardly Chekhov.'

'I know what you mean.' She sounded desolate.

'D'you feel you're being well-advised by Gertie?'

Long pause.

'Yes.' But this yes was said with the force of no-not-really, and didn't fool me.

'Well, then,' I said, taking in a long breath to help me get to the end of a long line, 'All I can do is say good and excellent. I'm really glad you feel like getting back to work. I just hope the play gives your talent the scope it deserves and that the cast is one you're going to enjoy being with for a long run. Anyone I'd know?'

Jess reeled off names, none of which I recognized but then I didn't know anything much about the commercial theatre. 'There is just one flaw: they don't want to pay me properly.'

'Is Gertie working on that?'

'I've told her she must. I'm not going up north and down south without incentives.'

'So, what's the position? Have you accepted? Signed a contract?'

'No!'

It took about ten days for the details to be sorted out and for Jess to be offered the fee she regarded as appropriate. By the time she got to her first fitting she was three weeks behind.

'Don't ring me! I can't speak to anyone. I've got to learn these bloody lines and they're impossible.' Her voice was almost unrecognizable. It was as if she had assumed an accent with which she was not born and in her hysteria was forgetting to use it. And Jess was studiedly courteous by nature. It was shocking to be confronted by an unrecognizable truculence. I remember thinking that this was where self-absorption went when the going got rough.

It was eleven at night when next she rang. She was virtually incoherent. Had it not been for the fact that Jess did not drink over and above the occasional ceremonial glass of Veuve Cliquot, I would have thought her drunk. The play was despondently naff. Why in hell's name had she committed herself? The cast were nice enough not to let down. What was she to do? She hated her costumes, they made her look like a transvestite brothel-keeper. She did not pause for breath. Would I go to Sketchley's and pick up ... and then to Boots and get her the nail-varnish remover for acrylic nails and send round a pizza and could I lend her my hair dryer, hers had packed up, and would I ring her accountant: 'I'll give you the number and tell him ...' On and on she rambled while I interrupted with the occasional 'Of course', 'Don't worry', 'Is there anything else?'

She rang off. Next morning at seven she rang. She'd been up all night and sounded worse than ever. She had forgotten to tell me they were opening in Brighton and she was going down five days early. They were only going to rehearse for two days. Not knowing anything about what was normal I did not express my fears that this might not give her enough time to feel settled in.

'Shall I come down for the first night?'

'I'd kill you if you did!'

'That's a big drastic, Jess.'

'Well, I'd certainly never speak to you again.'

'Where are you staying?'

'At the Grand. It's costing me more than I'm earning.'

And that was that. I wanted to say, 'Chuck it in, at once!' But those were not the lines for the role in which Jess had cast me. I was there to do as she wished and for a reason I could not then and cannot now fully explain, I accepted the limitations imposed by that role. I wrote her a note wishing her the best and took it to the local florist and ordered flowers to be delivered to the theatre on opening night.

∞

For a few months I had not been feeling well. Eventually, I made an appointment to see my GP who arranged to have some tests done. The results were inconclusive. I rang Yvonne and confided my anxiety. Our conversation was stilted. I wanted to avoid sounding hysterical; she was determined not to agitate me by showing apprehension. She must have felt she had not responded adequately to my predicament because I received a long letter from her, the opening sentence of which read: 'I want you to know I am truly concerned about you. I realize that the death of Jess must be a terrible shock to you and can't be helping to settle your fears about your physical health.' I read and re-read that sentence and just let my eyes gaze at the rest of the page without taking in anything but the word 'obituary' and the titles of three broadsheet papers. Pain stabbed me and I reeled. I was unrecognizably confused. Tears welled and my nose dripped onto Yvonne's letter. I felt my face burning and my limbs freeze. I thought: this is shock. I sat down and tried Yvonne's number. I kept getting it wrong and when finally I got it right it was her answering machine.

I assumed Jess had had a heart attack but as soon as that explanation satisfied me I started to wonder whether, perhaps, she had been involved in some sort of accident. The problem was, there was no one I could consult. It is one thing to commiserate with a stranger over a death affecting us both, quite another to interrogate the stranger as to the cause of that death. I kept remembering how well Jess was physically. I kept telling myself that one does not die of nerves.

The local library produced back copies of the papers. The obituaries had beautiful, out-of-date photographs of Jess. They gave her a splendid press: she had been 'sensational' in all sorts of plays up and down the country. She had died 'suddenly'.

Gertie and two of Jess's friends who knew Gertie made the arrangements. Amy rang me to say where the cremation would take place – and how Jess died.

She had killed herself, taken two hundred paracetamol on top of the uppers and downers she always took. She just could not get the badly-written lines of the play into her head. She had 'corpsed' repeatedly during the previews.

She killed herself because she was a control freak, and the role of self-slayer fitted her psychological make-up. She had not found the courage to approach her agent and pull out. Nor had she contacted a friend to confide the hole she was in and ask for help to dig herself out. As she probably saw it, that would place her under an obligation.

I was heart-broken. I had lost a precious friend late in life. I was indignant. If any show had to go on it was Jess's personal drama and not that of a miserable whodunit. There were things I had not understood about Jess. Her exquisite manners, even temper and glamour, which lent her such authority must have been masking a violence she felt that eventually emerged against herself.

And now she was taking the cruise she never wanted to take. Now she was abroad. Alone.

The Mistress

THE ANNOUNCEMENT of the forthcoming marriage of Melanie Lloyd to Miles Cardew was welcomed by all who knew the couple. Both Lloyd and Cardew families were more than satisfied with the choice their offspring had made; not only were the participants themselves charming but the families so suited to one another. Delightful additions to their respective circles. Melanie was beautiful and Miles was handsome and had wonderful prospects. Melanie's father forked out for a house in Chelsea for the couple. Miles's father, having first arranged for his son to acquire stockbroking skills in a large City firm, now took him into his own and made him a partner. The couple was set fair for a more than comfortable life.

Until she was four months pregnant with her first child, Melanie continued working on the fashion magazine she had joined after graduating with an inconspicuous degree. From then on, through the births of a further two children, she would occupy herself exclusively with the home and the needs of the little ones – and those of her husband.

But not all of Miles's needs. The couple had married young. Melanie was twenty-three and Miles twenty-five. The children arrived in quick succession and by the time Melanie was in her mid-thirties her hormones let her down. Despite her genuine and exclusive affection for Miles, the mere thought of that aspect of expression was anathema to her. She recognized she had a problem but not where she might take it. Certainly not to her GP. It was not as if she were ill. Miles was understanding – that was to be expected – but he was quite wrong in his judgement as to the cause of his wife's frigidity. He thought it was her fear of more pregnancies and despite his initial prejudice against the Pill, for the possible risks it threatened, he suggested to Melanie that she might take it for a while. 'See how you feel!' Melanie felt nothing but distaste and mounting guilt.

Miles was working long hours and making much more money than the couple needed. He was generous to his wife, imaginative with the children, responsible as regards provision for all their futures. He bought a house on an estuary in Hampshire, a holiday home from which they could sail. Whenever Melanie considered the lack of physical intimacy between herself and her husband her thoughts entangled themselves and she could make no sense of them. Miles was the perfect husband. She was utterly to blame for something over which she seemed to have no control. While some of her women friends complained about their husbands' excessive drinking, meanness, squalid personal habits, lack of consideration, Melanie could only produce a picture of Miles as the perfect companion.

Melanie kept her problem and the guilt it engendered in her to herself. However, she fancied it must have something to do with the fact that she and Miles were spending less and less time together. Miles was always exhausted when he got home from the City; he barely had the energy to say goodnight to Rosa, Hugo and Tertius and pour himself a drink, let alone indulge in conversation with his wife. His silence was not, however, hostile, Melanie thought. He had been talking all day; it was natural he should want to stop when he got home. That was probably why he seemed so indifferent to their entertaining old friends at home. Nowadays there always had to be an *occasion* to celebrate, an anniversary of some sort – or Christmas.

Miles was entertaining clients at restaurants – sometimes as often as three times a week. 'Do you prefer to entertain clients this way?' Melanie asked him. 'Indeed I do!' Miles assured her. 'I don't want clients invading my privacy.'

Melanie continued trying to work out why she felt numb. What were the reasons? But as soon as she started to think, her thoughts scattered. She was not analytical by nature. Her expectation of marriage was born out of her observation of her parents' experience. Like Miles, her father had been out of the house all day and was either exhausted in the evening or out entertaining clients (although her mother had more often than not accompanied him). At weekends he had played golf, walked the dog and read the papers. She could not remember her parents talking much. Unlike Miles, who did take an interest in Rosa, Hugo and Tertius, her father never did much with her or her sister. And Miles's interest in her appearance was quite unlike the apparent indifference her father showed to her mother, or his tight purse strings when it came to her clothes. Miles would always comment on what she wore and never on the sums she spent on her couture wardrobe. All in all, he really was the most excellent if not the most desirable of husbands.

But now Melanie had to face the fact that Miles hardly ever spoke to her. It was not that he ignored her, it was that he never initiated a conversation with her. And of course, he was frequently away. It had become a habit to spend one Sunday a month in Winchester with Miles's family and one in Selbourne with her family. But even these pleasant obligations were being eroded. The house on the estuary was seldom used at weekends. Melanie used it for the children's school holidays. When Miles managed to get down he sailed with the children by day and in the evenings went off to the club while Melanie played board games with her brood, or read.

Following one such long summer holiday Melanie noticed a dramatic change in her husband's mood. He had come down for one of the six weeks Melanie was staying. He was positively talkative, even jaunty – not a word with which Melanie would have thought to describe him in the past. Nothing seemed to have changed in the routine of their life, nothing Melanie could identify. When they returned to London he was out in the evenings as often as before, and well into the night. 'Just dining a client. I'll be late: he's a talker!' And Melanie registered it would not be necessary to have the table laid in the dining-room and three courses prepared. She would ring a friend and suggest they eat something together round the fire, or go to a cinema. 'Where's Miles?' 'He is entertaining a client.' One rather flighty divorcée did wonder aloud whether the client was male or female. The subject had never crossed Melanie's mind. 'All Miles's clients are male. What women do you know who manage their own portfolios?'

Melanie and Miles never referred to their problem, believing 'what we cannot speak of we must pass over in silence', but certainly not knowing who first had made the point and apropos of what. Nor did Melanie discuss her private life with old friends or the elegant acquaintances she made through her children, first at prep school and then at Westminster. She was seen by her contemporaries as devastatingly attractive, rather withdrawn (was she vain?), and the women tended to be envious of her perfect marriage. Even her children appeared unusually well-behaved and well-balanced. As much as Melanie held others at bay so the women took their cue and kept their distance. As for the men, with the instinct of animals they sensed they did not stand a chance with her.

Melanie's birthday loomed. She was to be fifty. Miles came into the dining-room where breakfast was laid and told his wife to pack a weekend bag for them both. The chauffeur would pick her up at three that afternoon, then collect him from the City office. No, he would not say where they were going. It was to be a surprise.

The Cipriani was a surprising choice for Miles to have made, Melanie thought. She would have preferred the Gritti . . . But she was certainly not going to say so. It was so unexpected of Miles to have planned all this. And the brooch he gave her over dinner was stunningly beautiful. Melanie knew from the glances she received that in her glorious Versace silk, with her jet black hair (not a single grey transgressor in its midst) her size twelve body and size four feet, shod in Monsieur Clergerie's best, she was looking as good as she was able. Miles was wearing a linen suit she had not seen him wear before – 'Armani,' he told her – and a shirt with a cossack neck and no tie. How youthful he looked! Melanie felt elated. She knew they would talk that weekend.

After dinner they took the private launch over the lagoon to seek out a little bar they had visited years ago, and sat drinking. Miles was full of what it was they were going to see over the next three days: the Carpaccios in that dimly lit, tiny church, the Giorgionis, the Titians . . . They would explore the labyrinth of alleys in this altogether enchanted city and rise at dawn to watch the first rays of dazzling sunlight on the Campanile. Miles had tickets to the Bellini at La Fenice. All this was just to whet their appetite for a longer visit in the future. 'We've been doing too little together, alone,' Miles said. 'Yes,' Melanie murmured, more to herself than to her husband.

Lying in the dark in bed, not touching, like two marble effigies on sanctified ground, Miles asked Melanie how she would feel if he were to move out of the house. She thought the question was hypothetical and answered that she would feel dreadful. But Miles continued in the same vein, pointing out that they never saw one another during the day and he did so much entertaining in the evenings, they hardly spent more than two or three nights together each week. Melanie said she would still feel dreadful, but recognizing that this matter was more urgent than she had at first registered, she asked Miles where he would go. 'To Frances, my mistress!' Melanie was too stunned to speak. 'You must have realized there was someone else. Surely, you knew I would *have* to have someone?' But Melanie never had realized that. 'I was sure you knew and were just too well-mannered to say anything. All those dinners with clients, those weekends golfing, those telephone calls late at night . . . Didn't you see through it all?' No, she hadn't. Not only was she inadequate as a wife, she was stupid. She was going to have to pay for both. She felt sick.

Miles told his wife that many years ago he had promised his mistress that when her elderly husband died – so long as his three children had left home – he would marry her. 'I promised. I always felt I was using her. Now the time has come for me to absolve myself from my guilt by honouring my promise,' Miles continued, telling Melanie that if she were to agree to the future he had mapped out for them they could be together just as often, if not more than in the past. 'We would spend two or three evenings a week either at some form of entertainment and then a restaurant, or at the house, whichever you preferred. I'd come down to the estuary once a month for the weekend. We'd go to your family and to mine once a month on Sundays, as we have always done; and instead of my being *absent* abroad, you and I would be taking those trips together. I really do believe we'd be seeing more rather than less of one another.'

Despite Melanie's lack of imagination regarding her husband's needs and their fulfilment, despite Miles's misplaced reading of his wife's imagination, their understanding of one another's behaviour patterns was reliable. Neither made scenes. Whatever the situation they behaved with courtesy. What neither foresaw was how turning Melanie into a mistress would alter their relationship dramatically.

Six months of being wined and dined, entertained at the theatre, the opera and the concert hall and being whisked off to Paris, Vienna and Rome for the weekend had had the most stimulating effect on Melanie's hormones. Miles telephoned Melanie at least twice a day. They talked at length. Miles bought his wife lingerie from Janet Reger and had exotic cut flowers and pot plants delivered to the house each week. Melanie had always been well dressed and well groomed, but only now did she start to pay attention to her diet, attend the gym regularly and have massage. Once every three months she spent five days at a health farm.

Miles had become a skilled lover. Quite different from the old days. Melanie wondered about Frances: was it to her that she own Miles's proficiency? She was too courteous to enquire.

All might have proceeded seamlessly had it not been that Frances was a woman of little perceptions and a conformist's view of marriage. She believed she had a right to know where and with whom her husband spent every minute of his time, his time being hers. Miles's refusal to play the game according to Frances's rules exasperated his second wife, and when Frances smelt *Joy* on his clothes, she exploded and lashed out with her fists and gave Miles a black eye. She wasn't going to be treated like his first wife! No way!

The subterfuge that was involved in Miles and Melanie keeping their arrangement from family and friends added spice to their situation. They laughed and joked together, imagining what people would think if they knew. It came as a revelation to Melanie that the role of mistress suited her so much better than that of wife. It came as a revelation to Miles that what aroused and interested him in Melanie were qualities for which he had not married her. They might have lived happily ever after had Frances not insisted upon a divorce.

A Different Country

BIRGITTA DUTHUIS, née Backhaus, accepted Dudley Farqueson's proposal of marriage in the spirit in which it was proffered, that of camaraderie. Dudley no more had at his disposal extravagant rhetoric than the passion with which to excite it. Birgitta responded in kind with a peck on Dudley's cheek, a winning smile and a brief tightening of her grip on his outstretched hand. The mood of affectionate companionship was to reign over forty years of marriage and three children.

Law and order featured high on the list of priorities in the Farqueson household. The whole family shared in the view that all was for the best of all possible worlds. Dudley had been called to the bar before he married. Little by little he became established and the couple moved from the large mansion flat in South Kensington to an architect-designed glass and steel house on the Thames, with mooring for a motor launch.

Birgitta fitted into life in Berkshire with the ease characteristic of many Danish women who live outside their own country. It is as if Denmark breeds into its citizens a chameleon quality enabling them, wherever they settle, to take on enough local colour to absorb them into the community and render them harmless, something which particularly suits the English of the Home Counties who are fearful of difference. The Farqueson children emerged blond of hair and blue of eye, tall enough to escape notice but to assure them the start in life denied to the short. Birgitta furnished the family home with Danish furniture, fabrics, china and glass. The effect she achieved was sunny, airy and hospitable, qualities which drew compliments from her neighbours.

When the children left home, Dudley and Birgitta did not think of moving house. They would end their days together where they had so successfully put down roots. Dudley would continue in his practice but for three rather than five days a week. The extra time for himself would be spent on the garden and the boat.

When the children were young, Birgitta used to take them to Denmark for the long summer holidays. She herself would return alone to celebrate her parents' anniversaries. Dudley was accustomed to her absences and instead of returning to an empty house would stay the week or ten days in his flat in St James's and indulge himself on more oysters and stout than was strictly recommended for his health.

Birgitta's measured temperament and habits were shattered the morning she received notification of the death of Fabrice Duthuis's wife. The black-bordered card printed not only the date of Chantal's demise but an invitation to attend her interment. On second reading, Birgitta realized that both death and burial had taken place two years past. Why had she been informed? Why now? She sat at her desk staring out at the river trying to remember Chantal. Was it once or twice that she had met her? She could not be sure. Her memory was frozen at the moment when Fabrice told her that because Chantal was, like him, a pianist, he had more in common with her than he had with Birgitta. He had fallen in love with Chantal, he said. It was best to be honest and say so at once. He had insisted she should leave. Soon. There was no point in dragging out an unsatisfactory situation. She would get over him. The two years they had spent together had not been entirely wasted but it was time to move on. The flat must be vacated. Chantal was waiting to move in.

Birgitta sat frozen at her desk. Notification of a death demanded immediate action. She felt she must write to Fabrice at once and express her sympathy. She felt none, but that did not absolve her from doing the right thing. She would keep her note formal.

How easy it had been to forget that short marriage! The impression left by two years with Fabrice was so faint as to seem to have belonged to someone else. She also remembered it had been 'passionate', although quite what 'passionate' felt like she could not remember.

Fabrice's letter, written in a shaking hand, thanked Birgitta for her sympathies and asked her to visit him: 'I am old and I am alone. I am physically unwell. It would be a great pleasure to have you with me.'

This second stab from the past was unsettling. At first Birgitta thought she might reply saying that family commitments were such as to prevent her getting away. Then, that she could not get away just now. There was more than something in Fabrice's description of himself that needled her. His might well be an accurate picture but it was clearly intended to appeal to her, as if she owed him something. However, it was rather winning of him to write that it would be 'such a pleasure' to have her with him. She observed – not without some discomfiture – that she experienced a little *frisson* of unfamiliar excitement.

Birgitta lied to Dudley, saying she was going to Paris for a few days to meet a Danish friend and do some shopping. She did not need to consider whether or not to tell Dudley the real reason for being away. She knew unconsciously that all that belonged to her first marriage was so out of keeping with her second as to make it unthinkable to bring the two together. It was only on the plane to Paris – limbo time – that Birgitta sought and successfully recovered details of her flight to and from that city forty years ago.

She had left her parents' guest-house on the Baltic intending to see something of the world before settling down, eventually, and taking over from them. She met Fabrice on the very train she boarded in Copenhagen. In the time it took to hurtle from Copenhagen to Paris, Birgitta had renounced a life of sober tranquillity for one of passionate chaos. Forthwith, she dedicated herself to soul-searching conversation and breathless love-making on a diet of music, Gauloises and Pernod. She swore eternal allegiance to the man without whom her life would be senseless and barren. Whatever happened – she could not imagine what, but felt it silly to tempt providence by seeming to assume too much good fortune – she would always be there for him. She made this the crux of her farewell speech. A year later she married Dudley.

Since leaving Fabrice, Birgitta had never visited the Boulevard Raspail where they had lived. Whether she had subconsciously avoided it, or simply had had no reason to be in that *quartier*, she could not be sure. But when she alighted from the taxi, the house appeared totally familiar and Fabrice's doorbell immediately distinguishable from the nine identical others.

When the lift came to a halt at the top floor, Fabrice was there waiting. He made no effort to help her open the lift gates but stood bent double at his front door. Once Birgitta had successfully extricated herself and her overnight bag from the lift's awkward gates, Fabrice threw open his arms and embraced her. Birgitta freed herself hastily and Fabrice stood aside to let her pass into the flat.

The heat was overpowering. Yet Fabrice was fully clothed – trousers, two sweaters over his pyjamas (visible at his neck and ankles), a woollen dressing-gown and a scarf wound loosely at his throat. His hair, now grey, had grown in long wisps to his shoulders. Birgitta would have passed him in the street without recognizing him. Surely, he had been exceptionally good-looking? Neat and tidy, with a passion for well-cut jackets and trousers and expensive shirts and ties. Once again, he took hold of her, this time at arms' length.

He examined her from her grey hair to her swollen feet. She sensed his disappointment.

'How are you?'

'Sad, lonely. Perpetually cold.' He turned to go back into the bedroom, Birgitta followed. She watched him slowly resume the prone position in which he spent his time.

Birgitta noticed how discoloured the sheets were under the expensive cashmere throws. The contradiction was somehow degenerate. In response to her glance, Fabrice said there was no need to change the sheets: 'No lovers these days.' Birgitta shuddered inwardly. Now her gaze fell on the three bottles of wine, the overflowing soup plate of cigarette stubs and the packet of cheap sweets that lay on the floor beside the bed. There was no space on the bedside table for these palliatives; its surface was piled high with tablets, potions, suppositories, phials and plastic syringes.

'Do you get out at all?'

'I'm too tired. I get up from time to time to relieve my back ache but there's nothing to keep me up.'

'And what about getting out?'

'Occasionally, to the brasserie, when I feel up to it.' He paused, as if further effort were beyond him. Then, following Birgitta's gaze: 'The caretaker's wife does odds and ends for me when she wants money for bingo.' Evidently the 'odds and ends' did not include any cleaning. Every flat surface was thick with dust. The carpet was wine-stained. The windows overlooking the crowns of fine trees were streaked with dirt. The clock had stopped.

'Do you read?'

'No, I can't concentrate. I watch the television.' Birgitta sat down on a chair festooned with items of Fabrice's clothing. She felt that to remove such items would be too intimate a gesture.

'Don't let me stop you!' she said, pointing to the television screen. Fabrice all too hastily pressed the remote control. Birgitta went back into the music-room.

The surface of the Steinway Grand was lost under sheet music and publicity leaflets. On the floor under the piano lay more scores, odd socks and shoes and plates with rotting apple and orange peel. A huge Chinese vase filled with masses of chrysanthemums stood on a marble plinth, the flowers so dead one jolt would have reduced them to powder. The walls of the music-room were shelved with recordings of Fabrice's recitals and concerts and interviews in French, German and English, meticulously labelled with date, location and names of those involved. There were framed certificates and medals he had been awarded, and photographs of himself at every stage of his career. Everything referred directly to celebrity. Birgitta remembered with the merest, wry smile the fortitude with which Fabrice had endured adulation. He had always felt well-satisfied it was owed him.

There was nothing of Chantal in any of the rooms. Even the kitchen, in which Birgitta was confident Chantal had laboured tirelessly, had no suggestion of her existence. Birgitta wondered of what Chantal had died. Neglect, perhaps?

Birgitta felt depressed and bored, out of place, almost an intruder. Why had she been asked to make this journey? Why had she agreed to it? Fabrice was acquiescent in his imprisonment with his mate, Death. She returned to his bedside.

'What is it you would like me to do for you?' she asked.

'There's nothing you can do.' He switched off the television and began to speak about Chantal. 'Beautiful Chantal!' An exemplary wife who had given up her career for his, preferring to attend to his needs than her own. No one could have entertained more gracefully than she, or kept from him more courteously the hordes of pestering fans. No one could have occupied herself with greater subtlety with matters relating to his agent, his recording manager . . . 'She sacrificed herself for me!' he said, 'Did I ask too much of her? Is that why my soul's in such agony? Am I paying the price of her sacrifice?' Tears dripped down his face. While he wept, it occurred to Birgitta that she had no option but to hear him out. She had been waylaid to witness his grief. His was a living death, intended to render her forlorn. She waited a decent moment before asking Fabrice whether he would like a cup of coffee.

'Weak tea!' he replied.

She was glad of something to do. Rummaging in the kitchen cupboards for tea and sugar, and in the fridge for a lemon, she discovered that all Fabrice's groceries came from Fauchon and Fortnum's. There were jars of caviar and tins of *foie gras* and wooden boxes of crystallized fruits and *marrons glacés*. It seemed somehow incongruous to nurture grief so extravagantly, so exotically. But the kitchen sink, loaded to its brim with dirty dishes and cutlery, quickly restored the prevailing mood of neglect.

Birgitta took Fabrice his tea. 'I'm going to clean the flat and then I'm going to prepare us some supper.' Fabrice looked up at her and nodded. 'By the way, do you bathe at night?' she asked, mindful of the limitations of the immersion heater.

'I don't bathe, *tout court!*' he replied.

Once Fabrice had swallowed four sleeping pills and turned off his light, Birgitta bathed. She was exhausted. She hoped the bed in the spare room was made up. It was. With linen sheets. She slid quickly between them, drawing the top sheet up across her face. She breathed in the warm cleanliness. A wave of exquisite pleasure broke over her. She could not account for it. It brought with it no hint of its source. She breathed in again. An explanation struggled to reach her consciousness, like a piece of music approaching its finale, labouring to retrieve its original key.

Charming

WHEN I WAS A CHILD I lived with my parents in a small market town forty miles from London. For all the influence that London had upon it, Denlow might as well have lain four hundred miles away. There was a theatre, but it was always on the verge of closing through lack of support and so it was never redecorated and always inadequately heated. There was a cinema, owned and run by an eccentric old lady whose taste was for Ealing comedies, Anna Neagle romances and Second World War escape dramas. Shortly after I left home for university, a boutique opened in the High Street. It called itself 'Dazzle' and sold tight, banana yellow unisex trousers, boob tubes and leopard jock-straps. It was as fiercely proud of having broken the mould of Denlow as Mother and her friends were opposed to it on the same grounds. The Wimpy Bar had blazed a trail a year before and galvanized Mother into action. But to no avail. For some reason, generally thought to be shady, Denlow Council let it through. I think Mother bowed to a sense of impotence in the face of an unyielding world over 'Dazzle'. I felt torn. I had all the shops I needed in Bristol. But the fact that Mother wanted Denlow to stay resolutely in the nineteenth century got on my nerves.

I went to the girls' school. The daughter of the local solicitor, Jane Hodges, was in my year. She was neither popular nor unpopular: she went unconsidered. So it came as something of a surprise when I overheard my mother remark to the doctor's wife how 'charming' she was.

'So polite! Rather an old-fashioned sort of girl. A real dear!'

'I entirely agree!' the doctor's wife murmured. 'I remember

girls in my own young day much like Jane.' After this I looked more closely at Jane to try and see what it was that took my mother's and her friend's fancy. I discussed Jane with my best friend, Alice. We decided that Jane was far too fat and clumsy and her bottom far too near the ground for her to qualify as charming.

'And she's prim, to boot!' Alice said.

'She's a prig!' I summed up.

I was standing in the kitchen licking out the cake bowl when I judged the moment ripe to ask Mother what it was about Jane she found charming. 'Jane is the sort of young lady who would never answer her mother back,' she said, arranging her lips in a tight sphincter. 'And' she continued, only loosening her lips for her words to emerge as flat as toothpaste from a clenched tube, 'there would never be any need to tell Jane how to conduct herself with boys.'

'She'd never find herself with boys!' I answered, my finger still busy in the cake bowl, happy to be able to combine honesty with the barb.

'Precisely! And do stop doing that! Jane would behave "suitably". At fourteen it is not necessary to find yourself in the company of boys.' Believing herself to have scored a bull's-eye, Mother wiped her hands on her apron and left the kitchen.

Because ours was a girls' school our conversation was almost entirely devoted to the subject of boys, but Jane did not participate in it. On Saturday nights when a mixed group of us went to the cinema to explore each other's chests and mouths, Jane never accompanied us. I only registered how absent she was from wherever we were because of the fuss Mother was making trying to get me into Jane's company.

'Why are you so daft about Jane?'

'I'm not daft, as you put it. I just feel Jane would make a nice friend for you.'

'I suppose you mean Alice isn't a nice friend.'

I don't think Alice is a good influence. Jane would be an excellent one.'

'Mother! Don't you think I'm old enough to choose my own friends? Jane's boring.'

Jane did not do well in her A levels.

'Poor child! Of course, she'd had to do so much in the home these past years.' My mother's need to find an excuse for Jane's lack of achievement far outweighed her inclination to express delight that I had done better than anyone hoped, and had no fewer than four places at university to choose from. 'If Jane's mother had lived and Mr Hodges had not been so poorly, Jane would have sailed into Oxford,' Mother assured me, and made a point of remarking to anyone else she could waylay. In the event, Jane did a diploma in business studies at the local poly and then went to work in her father's old firm as personal assistant to the junior partner, Peter Williams, a rather yellow young man known to suffer with irritable bowel syndrome and delight in numismatics.

I was in my second year at Bristol University and had not been home for six weeks.

'How's Jane?' I enquired of Mother, grateful for any subject we might share.

'She's fine. Really come out of her shell. I wouldn't be at all surprised if she and Peter announced their engagement at Christmas.'

'Isn't she a bit young to be thinking of marriage?'

'Not a bit!' Mother replied firmly. 'I think marriage is quite the nicest condition to aspire to.' I think Mother sniffed. I couldn't be absolutely sure.

I remember being struck how much the influence of Jane Austen in respect of marriage was felt by Mother. What Mother had to say about Jane could have been written about

Emma Woodhouse and her father. I was certain Jane would take her father into her marriage, as Emma had promised.

However, Jane was denied the opportunity to make that sacrifice. Mr Hodges died before the wedding. Mother wrote that Jane was married in blue and that she looked 'charming'. (I should mention here Jane's obsessive devotion to the colour blue. She never wore anything but Hodge-blue – a colour bypassed by nature – not that of a Mediterranean sky or an African lake, but a near relative of baby-blue, a distant relative of Saxe-blue, dusty and drab.) Mother did not elaborate much on the wedding. She said she sang in the choir and that Jane and Peter had hired the church hall for the reception and that she, Mother, had known all the guests (they were locals) except for Peter's sole relative, a maiden aunt. I gathered from the tone of Mother's letter that she felt a little let down by this wedding.

Mother and Father had never had much money. Father was a quantity surveyor and Mother just kept the house. Rather than lament their shortage of money, they expressed an almost indecent respect for those with plenty, and slight contempt for those with little. Mother rounded off her letter by reminding me of the sacrifices she and Father were making to keep me at Bristol and by hoping I was working hard and not 'frittering away your time amusing yourself'. She enclosed a letter Jane had delivered to the house, thanking me for the two antique rummers I had given her as a wedding present. 'Just like you,' Jane wrote, 'original!' She urged me to visit her in her new bungalow when next I came home.

Mother refused to accompany me.

'You go on your own. Two girls the same age! You must have so much to talk about.'

Jane served tea and Bourbons in the beige-walled sitting-room. The brown cut-moquette three-piece was so ugly I tried to avert my eyes, but to alight on what? Not a picture on the wall, not a flower in a vase.

'How's Peter?' I asked. Jane replied that he was under the doctor, and she was rather worried. 'They don't seem to be getting to the bottom of it.'

I thought it best in the circumstances not to enquire as to the symptoms. I asked Mother if she knew anything.

'Poor Jane!' Mother sighed. 'I believe there is something seriously wrong.' I could only think of the big 'C'. Then it crossed my mind that he might be being *bored* to death. Since I was not in the least concerned about either of them, I thought it would sound macabre to make further enquiries.

Peter died five years after he and Jane married. Jane had nursed him at home and everyone said she had done all that might have been expected, and more. It was a tragedy, they agreed, for such a young woman to find herself alone. Mother assured me that anyone as 'charming' as Jane would be bound to remarry 'eventually, after a respectful period of mourning, you understand'.

Jane's need to nurture was next satisfied by dogs – Yorkshire terriers, to be precise. I sensed in Mother a disappointment, verging on disapproval, when she discovered that Jane was short of money and needed to breed the animals for sale.

'She could always go back to work,' I suggested.

'Jane doesn't want to go back, she wants to go forward.'

I wondered in Jane's case what 'going forward' implied. Mother hoped the vet. He was about forty-five and unmarried and Jane saw quite a lot of him because of the dogs. When next I saw Alice I asked her if she knew the vet.

'Very nice chap. He's gay.'

'Don't bank on the vet for Jane, Mother, he's not the marrying sort,' I said, careful to stick to Mother's coded language.

'You do say that most unfortunate things!'

'It's not unfortunate, Mother, it's fact.'
'And how would your friend Alice be privy to this fact?'
'Evidently, it's obvious.'
'Not to me it's not.'
Well, I thought, there's no answer to that.

Mother worried that Jane had become too isolated. Her home was on the edge of Denlow, in a close of five identical bungalows built just short of the industrial estate. At the rear, where she might have made a garden, Jane kept grass for the dogs to play on, and foul. At the front she did nothing to soften the effect of the concrete on which her neighbours parked their Fiestas.

I sensed Jane's charm was becoming less luminous in Mother's eyes. It was as if Mother's plans for Jane were not proceeding along prescribed lines. But then Mother would surprise me by reporting an occasion upon which she and Jane had propped up each other's certainties to their mutual satisfaction, and I was led to believe things were well between them. For example, Mother wrote that she had bought herself 'a very smart new winter coat in the sales'.

'I'm so glad you treated yourself', I wrote, adding, 'I bet it's blue.'

'How *did* you guess?' Mother asked. No, she couldn't say where she and Dad would take their holiday because she hadn't had the opportunity to discuss it with Jane.

'Since you're going with Dad why don't you discuss it with him?' I asked on the telephone.

'You know what your father's like,' Mother replied, somewhat enigmatically.

'You should take Jane with you!' I suggested. Mother did not wince at my cheek. On the contrary, she replied that it was not possible because one of Jane's bitches was due to whelp the very week Dad had to take his annual leave.

The years passed. I went to live with my partner in the north of England. Some years Mother and Dad came up for Christmas, some years we went back to Denlow. For a long time no mention was made of Jane. Mother and I had less and less to talk about. In desperation one day I fell back on enquiring how Jane was. I noticed a pause before Mother said Jane was 'quite well, thank you'. It was the finality of the 'thank you' that alerted me. It needed an explanation.

'Jane has remarried,' Mother said.

'Oh, you must be pleased!'

'As a matter of fact, I'm not a bit pleased,' Mother re-arranged her shoulders.

'Why's that?'

'She's made the most unfortunate alliance. He's young enough to be her...' Mother trailed off. 'He's unemployed ... he drinks and smokes...'

'She must be madly in love, then,' I offered.

Mother found this suggestion so offensive, she ignored it. 'The trouble with Jane is that she needs people to need her,' Mother said, clearly delighted with her perception. 'I can't tell you anything more about him because I've never met him,' she added, forestalling any further questions. 'Now, dear, you tell me what *you* are doing and how *you* are!' I was stunned: Mother calling me 'dear'! Next thing she'd be telling the neighbours how 'charming' I was.

I had become the good daughter. With Jane in the doghouse, I was in the ascendant. Not a week went by when Mother did not enquire as to my state of health and my job, my partner's state of health and his job. She looked forward to visiting us or being visited. This reversal was so complete, I sought an explanation from the textbooks. I knew about the good breast and the bad breast, the shadow and the substance, but who had researched the good adoptee and bad natural child?

The funny thing was, I became depressed. The sheer responsibility of not letting Mother down got the better of me. Had it been within my power, I would have arranged a divorce for Jane and found her a new, suitably rich husband.

Crises. 1939

It was unusually hot. It was ironic, they said, that August 1939 was so fine, for war was imminent and then hot or cold, rain or shine it would not matter. The 'Crisis' had shut down London. The Germans and Soviets had signed a non-aggression pact and Parliament had been recalled to receive the Emergency Powers Bill. It was all too terrible to think about.

Mrs Georgina Lowes was not thinking about it. She was pondering more personal concerns. She dressed absentmindedly (but from habit, with attention to detail) in a navy linen blouse and white trousers. Before going down to breakfast, she picked up *The Times* from where the page boy had deposited it.

Mrs Lowes's daughter, Julia, had placed a deck chair well away from others on the private beach of the Grand Hotel and it was there that Mrs Lowes sat. But she did not read. She stared out over the ageing forehead of the English Channel for some time, then told her daughter to fetch her writing materials. Julia Lowes, aged fourteen, rose from the rug at her mother's feet and walked up to the beach hut twenty-five yards away. When she returned her mother did not acknowledge the writing case: she was examining her face in a looking-glass.

'This heat is ruining my skin!'

'You look very well, Mama!'

'I've caught the sun!' her mother objected, dropping her hand into the striped beach bag at her side and taking out a linen Garbo hat and a pair of sun-glasses.

༄

The spacious Edwardian dining-room was already busy

when mother and daughter took their seats for luncheon at the reserved table in the bay window.

'Come, child, we don't have all day! Make up your mind!'

'I think I'll start with the Charentais.'

'You know you don't care for melon!'

'Oh, don't I? You choose for me, Mama!'

'My daughter will have the *pâté de foie gras*. For me...' Julia did not listen further. She had thoughts of her own. Why does Mama confuse her taste with mine? The pâté will be too rich and I shan't be able to stop myself imagining the fate of the poor geese. Surely I like melon? Melon is cool, clean, fragrant and summery...

'Julia! Julia! You're dreaming, child!'

'No Mama, just wondering in which direction you would prefer to take your walk this afternoon.'

Mother and daughter exchanged few words over luncheon. Mrs Lowes had her gaze fastened out to sea as if searching for something. Only the interruptions of a waiter forced her regard back into the dining-room where she registered with approval the arrangements of delphiniums and the salt-white damask tablecloths and stiffly starched napkins.

'What a pity there's no one of your own age here this year!' she sighed.

'But there are the Gordon and Farleigh girls!'

'I mean suitable young people.' *Suitable*, that portmanteau word Julia understood to mean well-to-do, well connected. 'And you have been wearing that dress for two days!' her mother observed.

'But I love it so! You have such wonderful taste, Mama!'

'Be that as it may, people will think I have failed to provide you with an adequate wardrobe.'

'I'll change for your walk.'

'I'm not sure I shall be taking a walk this afternoon. I feel a slight headache approaching. I think I'll rest. You go along alone. I'd like you to post my cards and buy me some of Arden's face cream.' Julia sipped her coffee. Mama liked her to drink it black, without sugar, not what she would have chosen. 'Get into the habit while you're young!' she had instructed Julia. When mother and daughter rose to leave the dining-room, they were escorted into the foyer by the *maître d'hôtel* himself.

The village of Caborn-by-Sea lay half a mile behind the promenade where the Grand Hotel stood. It consisted of a post-office-cum-newsagent, chemist, butcher, grocer and greengrocer. And a village hall. A notice on the green corrugated iron village hall drew attention to the tennis heats to be played on the courts of the Grand Hotel during the last week in August.

When Julia returned with her mother's face cream she did not disturb her siesta. She went at once to her own room at the other side of their sitting-room and immersed herself in *Judith Paris*. Mama knew nothing of the *Herries Chronicle* but because Julia had borrowed the book from her school library imagined it must be 'suitable'. Julia left her door ajar, as Mama preferred, and was aroused from her book only by the tinkling of her mother's little handbell. She dropped *Judith Paris* at once, rang room-service and ordered afternoon tea.

Mother and daughter drank Earl Grey and ate fresh scones with strawberries and clotted cream on the balcony of their suite overlooking the promenade. The sun was ever shining, the gulls ever screeching. There were few promenading, fewer still on the beach, for it was being encroached by the tide. A man sat disconsolate on his tricycle, failing to tempt with his ice-creams. Another strolled along, holding on to multicoloured balloons no one stopped to buy. One or two stray dogs sniffed among the pebbles that met the promenade. Julia had watched this languorous scene from the same balcony for ten summers. There was something reassuring about things that do not change, she thought. When she noticed six men in white flannels emerge from the hotel, each with a tennis racquet and tennis balls hung in yellow nets, she drew her mother's attention to them.

'Look, Mama, the players are off to the courts!' Mama lowered her chin and raised her eyes over her sun-glasses and peered across the balcony rails.

'Yes,' she answered, drawing out the word, packing it with dread meaning Julia wondered at and could not fathom.

∽

'I shall dine alone this evening. Ring room-service for a menu and arrange to have your dinner brought up at about seven-thirty!'

Her mother's outstanding beauty and incontrovertible power formed a single quality in Julia's mind. A request was an order made in the name of that beauty. She fastened her mother's diamond and pearl necklace and with a soft brush designed for the purpose flicked a few blond hairs and dandruff dust from the neckline of her mother's dinner dress.

'Enjoy your evening!' her mother ordered Julia. 'You have your book and the wireless. I believe there's a nice concert for you to listen to. Don't wait up for me. I may play cards until late.' As she made for the door, Mrs Lowes almost forgot to peck her daughter good-night.

It was the waiter who suggested that Julia took dinner on the balcony. 'You'll be able to watch the people,' he said, 'Less lonely for you.' Julia was glad of this suggestion. After seven, the private beach was thrown open to the public. There the villagers congregated if the tide was low and if the tide was high gathered on the promenade. Her mother insisted that Julia was in bed by nine-thirty, but being on her own Julia was allowing herself a little licence. She stepped out on to the balcony and curled up in a wicker chair and watched the twinkling lights that hung in garlands the length of the promenade. Above the low voices of little groups she heard the sea sighing as it fell and the pebbles tumbling as the waves withdrew. This was how she would always remember Caborn. As she rose to go inside, she looked over the rails for a final glimpse. To her astonishment she saw her mother emerging from the hotel with a man she did not recognize. The man was holding her mother's ermine wrap; now he was placing it round her shoulders. For a split second he was letting his hands rest on Mama's shoulders. Julia's blood ran cold. She backed away to make herself invisible and watched furtively while her mother and the man strolled out of sight.

In the very early hours of morning Julia woke to the sound of the sitting-room door opening and Mama slipping into her bedroom. Julia felt discomposed; she wanted to go to her mother and get into her bed, and weep. She knew better, though, than to attempt such a thing.

Mrs Lowes slept late. Julia did nothing to disturb her. Over luncheon, she informed Julia that she had two tickets for the semi-finals of the tennis tournament. Julia answered by saying she had arranged to spend the afternoon with the Gordon girls. It was a lie.

Again Mrs Lowes told her daughter to order dinner in the suite and turn in at nine-thirty. Julia felt cold desolation. Something had happened to poison the roots of the intimacy she shared with Mama. Mama was keeping something from her and she could not ask what. It had to do with that man.

Julia complained to the waiter that it was too chilly to eat on the balcony. She was determined not to give in to curiosity, not to look to see whether Mama was with that man. She had no appetite. Not wishing to have to offer an explanation to the waiter as to why she had left her dinner untouched, she flushed fish, meat and pudding down the lavatory. Nor could she settle to read. And she didn't want to listen to the wireless. She knew she was not going to be able to sleep.

The telephone startled her. She was shaking when she picked up the receiver.

'Papa! How lovely to hear your voice! How are you?'

'I'll come up and tell you.'

'Really? How's that?'

'I'm downstairs in the foyer. I was just making sure you were there. Tell mama...' Julia interrupted her father, not wishing to have to tell him that his wife was absent and, perhaps, have him alter his plan to come up. Julia adored her father, who was all treats and laughter. She did so wish he would spend more time at home. But he was an explorer. Lately, she had heard him tell Mama that he was going to volunteer for active service, not wait to be called up.

'Does that mean Papa will go abroad to fight?' she had asked her mother who had answered, curtly, that she certainly hoped he would not be fighting on *English* soil.

Roger Lowes hugged his daughter.

'How brown you are, darling!' he said, holding her at arms' length, clearly delighted with what he saw.

'Have you dined, Papa?'

'Yes, my dear. I had something on the train coming down.'

'I don't think Mama was expecting you.'

'No, I was not sure I could get away. Where is she?'

'She said she might play bridge after dinner. She's bound to be up soon.' Julia was anxious to keep her father with her and for him not to go looking for Mama. But she was unaccustomed to spending a whole evening with her father. She did not know how to entertain anyone so unbridgeably grown-up.

'I think I'll pop down to the bar. You get to bed!' Yes, now that Papa was here, things would be all right again.

It was dawn when she woke. Something was horribly wrong. Frightened, she sat up in bed and listened. Her parents! Her father was actually shouting and her mother was weeping. Julia crept through the sitting-room to the door of her mother's bedroom and listened.

'Bloody bitch! My God! A professional tennis player! Sodding Hun at that! I'll make you pay for this . . . Wanton trash, all dressed up in your finery but nothing but a slut underneath it.' There were sounds of a struggle. A piece of furniture crashed to the floor.

'You're hurting me!'

'You don't yet know the meaning of hurt. You soon will!' Julia covered her ears with her hands as she stood shaking outside the bedroom door. Without preparation, she found herself opening the door, standing transfixed, watching.

'Stop it! Stop it!' she screamed. Mama was on her knees, her evening dress in ribbons, her pearls scattered over the floor. She had her hands raised as if in supplication. Papa's right hand was held aloft, primed to strike Mama.

'Stop it! Stop it!' Julia yelled. Papa did stop and Mama did struggle to her feet. So Julia allowed Mama to blindfold her with her hands and turn her round to face away and push her back into the sitting-room. Then Mama returned to her bedroom and closed and locked the door against Julia.

It was the third of September 1939. War would be declared in a few hours.

Will Dolores Come to Tea?

'Wouldn't you care to invite Dolores to tea one Sunday, dear? I would so like to make her acquaintance. Perhaps *she'd* be glad to meet her friend's mother . . . ? What does she do of a Sunday? I'd bake my ginger cake, your favourite. Does Dolores care for ginger? Or would she rather lemon? Most do. What d'you think, Kevin?'

Mrs Carter hardly expected her son to listen to her. She certainly did not expect him to answer. However, she had made up her mind that in the event of Dolores coming to tea, she *would* bake the ginger cake. The fact that she had been nagging Kevin to invite Dolores for well over a year, the fact that he had not produced a reason for not so doing was disappointing, but Mrs Carter did not understand by it that he never would invite her. Although she would not have expressed it thus, the ongoing subject of Dolores's possible coming to tea was as useful a means of communication between mother and son as the weather and the cost of living.

'She sounds ever so nice, your Dolores. Is she a *kind* girl? You've always been such a kind boy. Even as a little one you were thoughtful. You were the one to bother about the animals.' Mrs Carter paused reflectively. 'Does Dolores make you happy, dear? A mother likes to know her son is happy.'

Mrs Carter was preparing Kevin's supper. While she washed, peeled and scraped, she spoke her thoughts over the sink, through the picture window and out on to the twenty square feet of lawn and its borders of petunias, French marigolds and busy lizzies. 'The annuals are doing well,' she observed. 'Does Dolores like animals and flowers?'

Dolores was much on the mind of Mrs Carter that evening but any image of the young lady escaped her. Kevin had once advanced the information that she was about his height — five foot six inches — and said she lived behind the store in Kingly Street, the store whose windows Kevin dressed. Mrs Carter hadn't liked to persist with questions so reluctantly answered but from what Kevin had let slip she imagined Dolores was something in sales. 'You've been having ever so many late nights, Kevin,' Mrs Carter ventured, rather boldly for her. 'That Dolores certainly keeps you on the go!' Having been more daring than was her custom, she sought to conceal the indelicacy in a little cough. 'Nice, though, to have someone to share with. I used to enjoy the theatre myself when I was young.'

Kevin offered to do the dishes. Mrs Carter said she appreciated the offer but he'd been hard at work all day and it was her pleasure when he was in of an evening — rare these days — to do it for him. 'What's Dolores up to this evening? Gone to see her mother, perhaps?' On being told that Dolores's mother was dead, Mrs Carter was quite overcome. 'Oh dear! Oh dear! The poor, motherless girl! Does she have a sister to console her?' Kevin reassured his distraught parent that Dolores had several sisters.

Mrs Carter completed the washing-up, the drying, the putting away and the swabbing down with Kevin's confidence echoing in her head. Poor, dear, orphaned child! What a good thing she had a nice young man in her life. But when she went into the sitting-room, where Kevin was sitting watching *Food and Drink* on the TV with a glass of whisky in his hand, Mrs Carter tutted and tutted and enquired as to whether it was Dolores who had got him drinking? 'You never used to like the taste of the stuff.' Perhaps, Mrs Carter reflected, Dolores would rather a rum baba than a ginger cake . . . She would look up a recipe.

'My Kevin's got ever such a nice young lady!' Mrs Carter was hanging out the washing and calling over the wall to her neighbour who was doing likewise, seeing it was Monday and fine at that. 'They're going to Paris for the weekend. I think it's wise the way young people try one another out these days, you know, before making a commitment.'

Mrs Gorringe was less sure. 'If I'd tried out my Albert before I said "I do", I'd never have married him.'

'Oh, well, I'm sure it's all been for the best,' Mrs Carter opined cheerfully, back on automatic pilot. 'Look at your lovely grandchildren!'

Mrs Gorringe's grandchildren being unavailable for inspection at the time, she turned her attention to her neighbour's washing line. 'Your Kevin will want someone very particular with smalls if she's going to do them as well as you.'

Mrs Carter agreed, adding that since Kevin had been at his present employment, he had spoilt himself with silk boxers and cashmere socks, the very devil to keep nice. 'But he doesn't just spend on himself. He's ever so generous to me,' she added quickly, to avoid any misunderstanding. The two women went their separate ways, back into their kitchens, united in their thoughts: Kevin's smalls. Very natural in a young woman to buy fancy underwear, less so in a young man.

'Does your Dolores spend a lot on her clothes?' Mrs Carter asked Kevin, seemingly out of the blue but in fact as a result of continuous days of speculation. For once Kevin seemed anxious and willing to reply. He confirmed that Dolores was exceptionally well turned out for every occasion and he detailed the contents of her wardrobe. Mrs Carter luxuriated in descriptions of velvet and taffeta evening dresses by Elizabeth Emanuel, tailored jackets and trousers by Armani and DKNY, country tweeds by Max Mara. Dolores had a packed social life extending from charity and hunt balls and the opera at one end of the spectrum, to weekends in the country demanding Barbour, Burberry and green wellington boots at the other. Kevin reeled off the names of restaurants favoured by the Princess of Wales, for which Dolores required immaculate tailoring and soft leather from Italy and Spain. Unrecognized names and untold luxury created a world of glamour from which Mrs Carter knew herself to be permanently excluded. She was not resentful of this. She would not expect the Queen Mother ('dear soul') to invite her to Clarence House, either. She ventured to assume that Dolores must earn a very good wage, to afford the best of everything. Kevin explained that the management encouraged her by way of reductions in price to wear what was on offer in the store. He pointed to his own wardrobe, which Mrs Carter had frequently remarked was 'as good as the Prince of Wales's' and which Kevin said was 'much trendier'. 'Well, dear, you'd have a lot to keep up with if ever you had to change your job!' This sudden convergence with the uncertainties of life bruised Mrs Carter's voice.

Throughout the following months, Mrs Carter persisted in her attempts to get Kevin to invite Dolores home for tea. Kevin persisted in ignoring her efforts. Uncharacteristically, he had taken two holidays: one in Morocco, for which Mrs Carter had evidence in the form of a postcard depicting camels and sand dunes. Another in Thailand from which she received a depiction of a vast beach on which two young boys were excavating rock pools. No, Kevin said, Dolores had not accompanied him. He had gone with friends. Mrs Carter worried. 'I hope nothing's wrong, Kevin. I mean you and your Dolores still see one another and so on . . . ?' She hoped the 'and so on' would be understood. She did so want grandchildren. Kevin was quick to reassure his mother that he and Dolores remained every bit as dependent upon one another. 'That's all right then!' Mrs Carter settled to polish the silver plate teapot and pierced bon-bon basket in the fervent hope they might shortly be required for use.

Mrs Carter mentioned to Kevin that she was considering getting Fred, the odd-job man, to redecorate the sitting-room. Kevin, however, expressed a wish to do this himself, and to reinforce his determination pointed out how much money this would save. He would take his time, even devote some outstanding holiday days to the job. He came home with paint cards, samples of carpeting, curtaining and upholstery materials. He made charts. He agonized over what would go with what. 'He says while he's at it, he might as well do the whole place, do the thing thoroughly, give it a makeover, like they do on that TV programme,' Mrs Carter excitedly informed her neighbour. 'And you're going to give him a free hand! Let him loose all over the house?' Mrs Gorringe did not bother to conceal her horror. 'Of course I am. My Kevin's artistic, you see. He's got a gift that way.'

Kevin's craftsmanship was impeccable and there was not a drop of paint spilt anywhere but for where it was intended. The curtains, the carpets, the upholstery and the cushions were not to everyone's taste – particularly not to that of Mrs Carter and her neighbours – but all judged it 'different' and reassured each other that, given Kevin's job dressing the windows of that celebrated store in Regent Street, he must know better than they what was nice and what went with what. 'His young lady, Dolores, shares his tastes,' Mrs Carter told Mrs Gorringe by way of further justification and to shore up any doubt she had. '*We're* old-fashioned, you understand!' 'Speak for yourself!' Mrs Gorringe was not ready to have the well-tried tastes of Knights Drive questioned.

Little by little, Kevin made over number thirty-four in a style much his own, but of the moment. He 'let himself go' Mrs Carter explained, in the bathroom and the spare room.

But so far as the kitchen and her bedroom were concerned, she had been consulted and yes, she did like the results very much indeed. 'Of course, I wouldn't interfere with what he chooses for his own room.' Since none of the neighbours would ever enter Kevin's bedroom, his mother was not going to be faced with explaining or defending the life-size photographs of naked male bodies taken by someone she thought Kevin spoke of as Mr Maple. 'What d'you think your young lady will make of it?' Mrs Carter was both curious and anxious. Kevin said she would be bound to like it very much and he added that at least she would have nothing to get jealous over. 'Oh dear! Is she the jealous type, then?' Kevin did not say. For the first time, Mrs Carter was experiencing a twinge of anxiety regarding her son's beautiful, blond, expensively got-up friend, who shared his interests and his tastes but did not always take her vacations with him. Had they really been together in Paris, she wondered?

One thing no man wanted was a wife who made difficulties, one who was suspicious, who nagged and had ideas of her own. Mrs Carter knew this all too well. She had learned it the hard way. Mr Carter had been very decided in his opinions, and to keep the peace his wife had learned to fall in with them. Kevin had been the biggest bone of contention between them. Mr Carter objected to what he judged as his wife's weakness in conceding to every one of Kevin's whims. He was particularly aggrieved that Kevin eschewed football, preferring to sit indoors with his embroidery. 'You're encouraging him! You're making him into a sissy-boy! What does he do for exercise?' Mrs Carter pleaded with Kevin who agreed to play some tennis. 'That'll give him the exercise!' Mrs Carter told her husband. 'And he meets a nice type of person in the park!' she added, by way of inducement. She took Kevin to one side and told him it would be best if he didn't work his chair seats while his father was in the house.

'And do get your hair cut, dear! Your father's been on about that, too.'

Mother and son accepted the untimely death of Mr Carter with equanimity. They never voiced what were their feelings in the matter. 'My husband never understood the boy,' Mrs Carter confessed to Mrs Gorringe in a rare moment of openness. 'Mr Carter was a man's man, if you get my meaning.' Mrs Gorringe got it in one. Her husband had been the same: 'All beer and fags and football out of the house and laying down the law in it . . .' Not to mention the none-too-occasional slap when some domestic chore fell short of his expectations. A Kevin-type husband would have well suited her, come to think of it. 'He's sensitive, isn't he?' 'That's just the word!' Mrs Carter agreed. Sensitive.

Kevin said he would pick Dolores up in the car, the old Austin that had belonged to Mr Carter. Mrs Carter had not been permitted to drive during her husband's lifetime and since he died had lost the urge to learn. Once a month, on a Sunday after lunch, Kevin drove her to Tesco's. He'd done that last Sunday. Mrs Carter had known since then of Dolores's projected visit and had had time for the minutest of preparations. She had got down the best china from its inaccessible cupboard, buffed up the four silver teaspoons and sugar tongs and washed the perfectly clean Madeira tablecloth and matching serviettes, normally used only at Christmas. She planned to cut dainty cucumber and tomato sandwiches without crusts, lacy thin and slightly moist. The ginger cake remained the centre-piece but she would do a few iced fancies, just in case. 'I don't imagine it matters what I look like!' Kevin overheard his mother think aloud. But she did change from her overall into a flowered skirt and blouse and her white shoes, 'seeing as how it's summer'.

Kevin was always stylishly dressed. That Sunday he was wearing a pair of light grey linen Nicole Farhi trousers and a matching but darker grey linen shirt. His new Cox shoes with wedges added a good two inches to his somewhat challenged height. He had sprayed himself in an Italian fragrance that combined the scents of leather and cardamom in a most exotic *mélange*. Knights Drive would have neither seen nor smelt anything like it had it been peeping through the nets at the open windows. However, since it was Sunday, the residents were either mowing the back lawn or washing their Escorts.

Kevin parked the ancient Austin up against the garage doors where no one could have seen what he was taking from the back seat. Anyhow, whatever it was was concealed under sheeting. He opened the side door to number thirty-four soundlessly and slipped into the dining-room unseen and unheard. Mrs Carter had laid the table for afternoon tea and had fled upstairs to apply dabs of talc to her flushed cheeks. Kevin unwrapped Dolores, unfolded her arms and legs and sat her on a chair. He straightened out her legs to fit under the table and adjusted her arms so that her hands lay either side of her plate. He set he head at a somewhat coy angle and ran his fingers through her gold curls. He had dressed her in white sprigged muslin from a Swiss house and wound wide, pink velvet ribbons about her waist. He stood back while he took corals from his pocket and then he fastened them at Dolores's neck and wrists. He had made up her face with fresh summery foundation, blusher and lipstick. He was well satisfied with his creation. He looked around the dining-room at the ambience he had prepared for her: it suited her and she it. It was fitting that his mother had got down the bone china and buffed up the silver, albeit plate. He went to the bottom of the stairs and called up, 'Mother, Dolores is here!'

Mrs Carter picked her way downstairs carefully. She had not worn the white shoes since last summer and they were tricky. She went straight into the kitchen, where the kettle was singing its readiness, and made tea. She picked up the tray, satisfied herself that she had remembered everything that was required and carried it into the dining-room. As she came through the door she caught the merest glimpse of Kevin's ravishing lady friend but because she was concentrating on not slipping – and on putting down the tray on a rubber mat so as not to mark the polish on the sideboard – it was no more than the merest glimpse. Only when she had patted everything in place did Mrs Carter turn to face her guest. 'My dear!' she started. She had had it in mind to say how much she had been looking forward to making Dolores's acquaintance, having heard so much about her, but in the event her voice failed her. Rooted to the spot, her prepared speech got stuck in her throat. She blinked several times in the direction of Dolores. And now she felt unsteady on her feet so she grasped the back of a chair with her two hands. He breath was coming too quickly. She knew she must make an effort to control it by breathing deeply half a dozen times. 'Dolores!' she managed, 'I am so very glad at last to meet my Kevin's closest friend. I hope you like ginger cake and iced fancies and old-fashioned sandwiches!' Stepping carefully, aware of the perils of her summer shoes, Mrs Carter circled her dining-room table to plant a kiss on Dolores's cheek. 'There!' Then without so much as glancing at Kevin she took her place at the head of the table and poured tea. For three.

The Return

LEV SAT AT THE EDGE of the raised footpath, his feet in the gutter. He held his head between his hands and looked down at the rivulet of rain coursing downhill under the bridge of his scratched knees. His brother's discarded boots were two sizes too large for his feet and had filled with rain. He was wet from head to toe: wet through. His hair was matted to his head and drops of rain slipped down his forehead into his eyes and mouth. He shook himself; he tried to free his thin, frail body from the clammy embrace of his shirt. He could not remember what it felt like to be dry, but he remembered it was better than this. He could not remember when it had not been raining. His arm ached horribly. But at least it was still attached to his body. That was a good thing. When the boys had swung him round and round he thought they might tear it out, take it home with them, eat it.

Lev took a piece of paper from his pocket, rolled it into a ball and dropped it between his knees. He watched as it was hurtled downstream braked by a boulder and beaten to a pulp. He got up. As he did so the too-large, uncontrollable boots dropped with a thud into a puddle and threw up mud over his legs and short trousers. Slowly, he shuffled the twenty-five yards home. The clouds were hanging so low that the houses appeared roofless, yet these houses on the edge of Spoltz were only one storey high.

Lev stood looking through the window of his home. A faint yellow light flickered. He stared at the front door, at the *mezzuza*, at the peeling brown paint, at the sign: 'Bar-Lev Carpenter. Tables, Chairs, Chests, Coffins. You name it!' He threw open the door.

'Mother! Mother! Little Mother! Where *are* you?'

'Here, my son!' Lev rushed to his mother's skirts and buried his head in the heavy black drapes that hung to the ground around the ample maternal form.

'You're soaking, my son. We must find you dry clothes.' She tried to disengage from the boy's clammy arms, but he would not let go. As she walked across the room, the room that served as kitchen, sewing-room, parlour and meeting-house, towards the fender on which a pile of clothes lay drying, Lev's mother carried her last-born on her feet.

'This is how frogs behave, Lev, not boys of ten and their mothers!'

∞

Two men and two women alighted at Llandornic station. As the guard slammed shut the train doors and blew his whistle, the two men were already mounting bicycles, cycling off in the direction of the church spire, and one of the women, the younger one, was walking briskly in the same direction. But the middle-aged woman, who had descended from the train with some difficulty, lingered by the ticket collector, and only when she was confident that she had his undivided attention did she anxiously enquire of him whether Mr Lloyd was available to drive her to Gwyn Conwen. The ticket collector, four tickets in hand and a look of professional know-how all over his face, walked on to the forecourt of the small station.

'Dai! Dai!' he called out, in lilting Welsh cadences. But there was no reply. 'His taxi's here all right. He'll be back soon.' The colourless woman traveller seemed lost; she stood with a bag at the end of each arm, as if stationed in a lifelong queue and – although she was not in the normal way remotely interested in animal behaviour – watched as a bruiser of a black cat strolled slowly but purposefully from one side of the forecourt to the other and slid under a fence and into a field.

The rain had stopped. The air was filled with the scents of nuts and dead leaves and wood-smoke, and the sound of birdsong. Miss Gluckstein stood staring at the hills that rose in a circle round the Llandornic valley. But as she stared her being did not fill with loving tenderness and intimations of a spiritual kind; she did not assess what her eyes beheld. How could she? For all but four days in the year Miss Gluckstein was confined to a one-room flat in central London, hemmed in by livid red brick and grey concrete, her ears assailed by the sounds of lorries, buses and fire-engines by day, and drunks brawling by night. Her nose was acclimatized to petrol fumes. Indeed, all her senses accommodated the texture of the city, for they had been schooled on the route she had followed from Whitechapel to Stamford Hill to Holborn. Miss Gluckstein did not feel for the country, she never yearned for it. Thrust into its midst she was confused by it and felt disorientated by its apparent profligacy. She felt at home in Marks & Spencer, the public library (reference section), and the office where she worked.

Miss Gluckstein was the senior welfare officer, the very cornerstone of the Jewish Council for Refugees. She was imbued with the grim sense of imminent disaster appropriate to a servant of the Jewish community. In keeping with her job and her mood, she habitually wore brown and beige. But she kept a black outfit cleaned and pressed in her wardrobe, for black was the colour most often demanded by her leisure-hour activities: committee meetings on reparations, conferences on Soviet Jewry, fund-raising galas in suburban town halls and, of course, funerals and memorial services. Had she been asked (and she never had been) Miss Gluckstein would have confided to her interlocutor that life was a serious business, that hunger and poverty and danger stalked every corner, but that she was among the fortunate: Britain had given to her father, and thus to her, a nationality to be proud of, and a race of tolerant men and women to live among. And the Jewish Council for Refugees had provided her with the opportunity to serve her particular community.

'Dear Miss Gluckstein. What a good woman she is!' intoned the rich 'ladies', who did a little charity work on the various committees over which Miss Gluckstein presided. But Miss Gluckstein was not a good woman. She had never wrestled with her conscience, she had never had to choose between personal happiness and service to others. Not once had her honour been at stake, not once had the lure of personal fulfilment been extended in her direction. She had done as her father, Rabbi Gluckstein, instructed. She had never questioned his wisdom. He was a rabbi, his career was wisdom. And he was her father: he knew best. He was older, he was to be obeyed. Serving the community was an obligation, and if it could be said of Miss Gluckstein that she approached her obligation with no more enthusiasm than the average Harrovian his cold baths, the satisfaction was probably more complete in her. The joyless pursuit of character was a concession the rabbi made to life in Protestant England. He had insisted upon it in his daughter.

But the roots that had led Miss Gluckstein to the forecourt of Llandornic Station in the autumn of 1970 had long passed from her memory. Habit filled the space youthful rebellion might once have threatened. Miss Gluckstein did not know that the daily ten-minute walk she made from her flat in Southampton Row to her office in Mecklenburgh Square was accomplished with a heavy heart: all she had ever known was a heavy heart. From nine o'clock on Monday mornings until sundown on Friday afternoons Miss Gluckstein consoled the stricken and the displaced in the Jewish community. She visited Jewish geriatric wards and Jewish pensioners' homes. She kept in touch with those who had been washed up in mental institutions and were obliged to eat pork or go hungry, and neglect the Sabbath. In deference to their unhappy plight she herself ate bacon (but not shellfish), and travelled by London Transport on Saturdays. And recently she had added to her case load drug addicts. Imagine! she had exclaimed to her secretary, they were not only marrying 'out' on an unprecedented scale these days – not to mention experimenting with sex before they did so – but some (mostly, it had to be said, residents of the Kensington and Chelsea districts) were smoking pot! Miss Gluckstein's forbearance was under strain; she had even, on rare occasions, regretted the Almighty's generous decision to keep her alive long enough to witness such terrible goings-on.

Among her duties, Miss Gluckstein numbered four visits a year to a Mr Lev Bar-Lev who, quite unlike the rest of her flock, had elected to live half-way up a Welsh mountain. Alone. Miss Gluckstein made no bones about it and admitted to her colleagues that she was thoroughly irritated by Mr Bar-Lev's choice of location. It was difficult of access in fine weather and sometimes actually cut off in winter. She also admitted to being disappointed that Mr Bar-Lev had not responded to her suggestion that he introduce himself (or allow her to introduce him) to the Jewish communities in Swansea and Cardiff. On each of the occasions she had attempted to broach the subject Mr Bar-Lev swiftly and effectively turned the conversation to a less contentious one, selected by himself. Miss Gluckstein recognized in her client a man unable to fend for himself, and desperately in need of a good woman to do so for him. In addition to this selfless observation she had a more selfish consideration in mind: if Mr Bar-Lev would visit, or be visited by, some kindly soul from Cardiff or Swansea, she would not be obliged to undertake the uncomfortable, tiring and time-consuming journeys herself.

For his part Mr Bar-Lev was used to Miss Gluckstein and had no intention of so much as considering the possibility of a different welfare officer broaching his defences. If the Jewish Welfare pension he received was dependent upon someone checking up on him, he would tolerate Miss Gluckstein but certainly not someone new. It was not that he liked Miss Gluckstein, or looked forward to her visits, which caused an unwelcome interruption in his routine, but he was accustomed to her and them. He had come to regard her as a sort of punctuation mark at the end of a three-month paragraph. And somewhere in the bowels of his being, Mr Bar-Lev found reassurance in her fidelity: *she* had not wiped him from the slate of world Jewry.

'Ah! He's coming, now!' The ticket collector spotted Dai emerging from the field, buttoning his fly.

'Dai boy! You've got a fare!' With his left hand Dai continued to button, with his right he shook Miss Gluckstein's hand warmly. He opened the passenger door for her and drove off quickly, raising a shower of gravel, without so much as asking in what direction his passenger wished to travel.

Once the spire of Llandornic church had vanished from his rearview mirror and they were in open country, Dai observed how time had flown and could it really be three months since last Miss Gluckstein had visited? She assured him it was even a little longer, and fell to silent remembrance of the fawn Crimplene she had worn last time, and how she had felt chilly in it.

'I came in June,' she told Dai, adding that a crisis in the office had prevented her returning in September. There had been no crisis, since crises did not occur in Miss Gluckstein's office, but there was no point in explaining to the Welsh Methodist taxi driver that Yom Kippur and Rosh Hashanah fell in September.

'I had no cause to worry about Mr Bar-Lev. He was cashing his cheques regularly.'

A stranger overhearing such an intimate disclosure of Mr

Bar-Lev's circumstances might have been surprised and even affronted, might have regarded it as something of an indiscretion on the part of the social worker. But the fact was that Dai's mother was the local postmistress. It was to her that Miss Gluckstein sent Mr Bar-Lev's monthly cheques and it was she who held them for him to collect, together with his post office book into which the money was paid.

'Mother says the old man's become terribly vague. He trots into the post office all eager but by the time he's had a talk with Mother he's forgotten what he's come for, and then he leaves his money on the counter, and she is forever chasing after him . . . Evans says it's just the same in the shop. Mr Bar-Lev buys what he needs and then leaves everything in a heap on the counter. And I know he's having trouble controlling his dog: it's been sheep-worrying. The old farmer on the south side of the hill threatened to shoot it – and the old man. He got very upset, he did.'

Miss Gluckstein relied on the information supplied by Dai and his mother. She noted it down on her pad. Later she would slip the pages into Mr Bar-Lev's file.

Mr Bar-Lev had been receiving a subsistence pension from the JCR since arriving in Britain twenty years ago. The money barely covered his heat, light and food. Mr Bar-Lev did not qualify for the old-age pension, and would have been unequal to negotiate with the DHSS for supplementary benefit. He had no relatives in Britain (he was not sure that he had any elsewhere), he was unable to earn enough on which to live, and he had no savings. He had never been driven by an urge to make money, he had always just survived. From time to time he contributed articles in German and French to academic journals. In payment for these he received a copy of the journal and a couple of offprints and a reprimand for having typed his contributions on the backs of used sheets of paper. He did not worry about making a living.

Since arriving in Britain supporting himself had not been an option open to him.

Lev Bar-Lev was engaged on a life of Sabbatai Sevi, the false Messiah and Holy Sinner. He had started this work in his twenties, fifty years ago in Paris. He had had to abandon it during the war, when he was in hiding and had no access to research materials. In the late 1940s he had the great good fortune to meet the Welsh theologian Caradoc Vaughan in Paris. Vaughan had invited him to Oxford and arranged a Fellowship for him of three years' duration. When the Fellowship had run its course he had lent Bar-Lev the cottage in Wales, so that Bar-Lev had a roof over his head while he completed his work. Sixteen years later the work was still unfinished.

Caradoc Vaughan's relationship with Bar-Lev had been confined to matters relating directly to the subject of Sabbatai Sevi. He had regarded Bar-Lev's work as important, and had been impatient to observe what effect his interpretations of Sevi's life would have on the theological world. But he had not been much of a psychologist; it had not crossed his mind that Mr Bar-Lev was constitutionally unable to complete his work until he felt within reach of the end of his life. Bar-Lev's work was his life, as much – if not more – part of his existence as the two frugal meals he forced himself to eat every day, the bath for which he could afford to heat water once a week, and the weekly journey he made down the mountainside to collect his money and buy his food.

Mr Bar-Lev's routine was unswerving, to the point of being rigidly inflexible. Had he been forced to change it he would have suffered severe disorientation. It was only the fact that his body reacted like that of an automaton in the performance of basic practical matters that kept Mr Bar-Lev the port side of sanity. But there were times when days passed without his noticing, when his work was so absorbing that he did not seem to need food. Miss Gluckstein and Mr Bar-Lev were, in their separate ways, both slaves to routine. If they were antagonistic at a superficial level, at some deeper level they were tolerant of one another: both had been shaped by their fathers.

The JCR were not united in their thinking about Mr Bar-Lev's work. On the subject of Sabbatai Sevi they were almost unanimous in their hostility, but some feared more than others that if Bar-Lev's work received publication there might follow a revival of interest in a figure best forgotten. It was known that Bar-Lev regarded the followers of Sevi with sympathy, and the man himself with respect. It was also known that he was critical of the varieties of Judaism practised in England and America – a Judaism of convenience in which the worship of materialism was cemented in moralizing that righteousness was profitable and profit was righteous. It sickened him with its in-built assumption that God favoured the rich. He loved the popularism of the medieval mystics, the robust way in which they enjoyed their simple lives and their indifference to worldly success. Most members of the JCR consoled themselves in the belief that Mr Bar-Lev's work would never be completed. A handful paid lip-service to his work, out of respect for serious scholarship – and serious they knew it to be: at least three Oxford medievalists had lent their names to support Bar-Lev's Fellowship. However, the fact that not one of those was a Jew did give pause; it was hard for members of the JCR to assess whether this was a good or bad sign, and almost Talmudic exegesis was applied to the question. Among the reasons (unknown to members of the Jewish Council of Refugees) the Oxford men had for lending support to Bar-Lev's work on Sevi were his knowledge of Freud, his interest in Jewish folklore – with which he had an encyclopedic familiarity, evidenced by the weighty book on the subject he had published in France in the

1930s — and the dazzling imagination that characterized his pre-war fiction. Anyone, they argued, could write a biography, given a taste for research and an appetite for truth, but a biography that recreated its subject needed just that quality of imagination for which Bar-Lev had been celebrated.

The JCR were puzzled by the interpretation of 'imagination' advanced by the scholars who so ardently supported Mr Bar-Lev's application for financial aid. Miss Gluckstein and her immediate superior believed it was this quality which had driven Mr Bar-Lev to live like a tramp, to be so conspicuously un-Jewish in his personal habits. Neither was able to name a single Jew from the past, or indeed from the present who, like Mr Bar-Lev, lived half-way up a mountain without benefit of company other than that of a half-breed sheepdog, and seemed not to know the day of the week — or care to know, even if it was the Sabbath. It was understandable, they agreed, that given his history of wandering throughout Europe, Africa and America, he had long since abandoned the dietary laws, but not to know the day of the week, even when the bells of Llandornic church were ringing over the otherwise soundless hills, was singular. In this opinion they were joined by poor Mrs Lloyd, the postmistress. It made her quite nervous to see Mr Bar-Lev banging on the locked doors of the post office as she hurried to chapel, hoping to collect a cheque because he thought it was Friday.

'But Mr Bar-Lev, don't you listen to the wireless?' How could he? The batteries had expired and he had forgotten to replace them. Where were the ones Miss Gluckstein had brought along last time? Where could they have got to?

Dai's taxi stopped at the point where an unmade lane joined the narrow road from Llandornic to Gwyn Conwen Miss Gluckstein rolled down her fabric glove and rolled up her sleeve and consulted her watch. She asked Dai to return for her in three hours.

Dai drove off in the direction of the village two miles away on the shores of a reedy lake. As he got out of his taxi he looked back towards the mountain. Mr Bar-Lev's cottage appeared as a white stain on the green canvas. By the time he turned into his mother's cottage, next to the post office, Miss Gluckstein had not yet trudged half-way to her destination.

Her bags were getting heavier and heavier as she laboured up the lane. A dog barked. A curl of smoke was rising above the hedge. The old man must have fuel. Perhaps he had bought some. Perhaps he had gathered it. The dog barked and barked. Miss Gluckstein was as enamoured of dogs as she was of the countryside. To her a dog was not man's best friend but the source of foul-smelling excrement which gathered on the soles of her shoes. She regarded the present barking as excessive. Had she not previously made the acquaintance of Mr Bar-Lev's canine company she might have been more apprehensive, but not only did she know Adler's bark was worse than his bite, she could judge from its persistence that he was presently chained to the post at the door of the cottage.

It was a relief to let drop her bags. She knocked loudly with her knuckles against the cottage door. There was no response, but the dog wagged his tail enthusiastically and sniffed excitedly under Miss Gluckstein's skirts. She was glad there was no one around to witness the dog's lewd behaviour. She knocked on the door again, and, since there was no response, she quietly lifted the latch and peered in. Mr Bar-Lev lay sprawled asleep in a huge footless armchair. The clothes line on which his washing had been drying had snapped, and washing festooned his sleeping form. The whole room was steamy: the wood-burning stove was efficient and the drying woollen garments made the air inside the cottage quite as damp as that in the hedgerows along the lane. The sink was filled to overflowing with dirty dishes and used cutlery; the refuse pail was spewing out cartons, tins and boiled bones. A smell of decay filled Miss Gluckstein's nostrils and forced a grimace. Under the steamed-up window, and running the length of the wall – the plaster of which was falling away in patches of constructional acne – a trestle table was piled high with books and littered with papers. Miss Gluckstein's attention was riveted by the sight of a brand new passport which rose out of the chaos as bright as a diamond set in mud. Not wishing to be discovered prying she crept back into the lane, closing the door soundlessly and (with the dog once again taking an all-too-intimate interest in her skirts) knocked again. Her more frenzied banging roused the old man and she heard a faint 'Come!', and she entered.

Had he been physically capable of so doing Mr Bar-Lev would have risen for his visitor. His manners had once been elegant: he had always risen when a woman entered the room, taken her hand and raised it to within two inches of his lips; always opened the door and let her pass in front of him. Habit had rendered many of his gestures automatic and today, rather bent, he contrived to stumble over his visitor's legs, bag and skirt. Furthermore, he found himself caught up in a cat's cradle of washing line and articles of underwear, the sight of which he was unaccustomed to share with another. Thus occupied with the dual tasks of trying to free himself from his bonds and conceal woollen vests and long underpants down the sides of the armchair, he was able to accord Miss Gluckstein only the most perfunctory of welcomes. But if he could not take her hand to mid-chest, he could none the less welcome her with his voice. This he did effusively.

'My dear Miss Gluckstein, my guardian angel, forgive me! I appear to be somewhat tied up!' And he laughed, pleased to be able to summon the English language in a pleasantry. 'Please take off your coat and make yourself comfortable!' This last suggestion was hardly feasible, but Mr Bar-Lev was oblivious to the fact. As he struggled to free himself from a miscellany of grey woollens, Miss Gluckstein took off her coat and hung it on a nail behind the cottage door. She unzipped the simulated leather bags she had carried wearisomely up the lane and took from them a range of provisions not normally stocked by Welsh village grocers: pickled cucumber, salt beef, egg noodles and matzos among other things. From a pocket in one of them she drew a periodical, *German Life and Letters*. Mr Bar-Lev fell upon it avidly.

'How thoughtful you are!' He ordered Miss Gluckstein into the armchair from which he had by then managed to extricate himself. He announced his intention of making tea. He fussed around the chair, brushing from it biscuit crumbs, dog hairs and a sheet of ochred newspaper, then mustered his full concentration for the task of tea-making for Miss Gluckstein.

Mr Bar-Lev was not accustomed to company or to making conversation, but the habit of courtesy required him to face his guest when he asked her how her health was and what sort of a journey she had endured. These niceties, entailing the turning of his head from the task in hand, distracted him from locating the packet of tea he was sure was somewhere, the lemon, the knife with the serrated edge. Eventually, struggling, he succeeded in putting the kettle on the Calorgas hob. He then turned to try and salvage the knife from its position under a pile of dirty plates in the sink, where it lay rusting.

Bar-Lev could not be accused of living in the present, in one sense of that expression, but in another, mystical sense, he was doing just that. Judging from his appearance, he was not conscious of his own times at all, and the village children judged him 'loony' on the grounds that very often he arrived in the village wearing his pyjama trousers, kept more or less in place with string. Unknown to himself Bar-Lev mumbled ceaselessly when he was on his own – or judged himself alone. Anyone able to understand the complexities of his utterings (plus half a dozen European languages) would have heard a unique mosaic of medieval thought. On the Welsh hillside it was the sheep who took no notice of Mr Bar-Lev, in the village it was the cottagers, but the children could not ignore his mumbling: they attempted imitations and danced round him, tauntingly.

'Megan! Will you come inside *at once!*' a mother called to her daughter, seeing what she was about. 'And you too Wynford!' The adults observed that Mr Bar-Lev was not quite like themselves.

'Well, he couldn't be, could he? You'd not expect it, his not being one of us!'

Bar-Lev had never felt one with anyone. Since earliest childhood in the Jewish ghetto in Spoltz, where he and his fellow Jews had been made to feel like an unlanced boil on the flawless face of Poland, he had felt alien. And as he wandered the world he found he could only identify with the outcast, with those rejected and despised communities: the Blacks in southern Africa, the negroes below the Mason-Dixon line, the Algerians in the poor suburbs of Paris. But in his mountain retreat in Wales his strangeness did not present a threat. The villagers, he knew, noted he was different – a poor scholar with a thick accent, and with different concerns from theirs. But they were not hostile. Indeed Bar-Lev was confident that were he to be in danger from outside the immediate community, the villagers would protect him. Mrs Lloyd and her son clearly accepted that Mr Bar-Lev was unequal to maintaining himself, and needed the regular – if infrequent – visits from a social worker. They did not know anyone else as bereft of relatives and friends. However, his courtesies outweighed his eccentricities, even if it could be distracting in the post office to have to put up with the drone of his mumbling.

The fact that Mr Bar-Lev was a Jew in a largely chapel community was hardly a bad mark at all, and the fact that Caradoc Vaughan had bequeathed him his cottage a very good mark indeed. It was reassuring to observe that those who did make contact with the old man were the theologians – even if some belonged to the Anglican church. At least the old man was not ungodly.

Miss Gluckstein accepted the lemon tea but declined the bread and cheese. She could not help noticing that a bluebottle had made itself comfortable on the cheese, but reflected that at least the water had been boiled. The mug into which Mr Bar-Lev was poised to pour her tea was soiled. The old man took a tea-towel that had clearly done double duty as a floor-cloth, and wiped it. Miss Gluckstein felt sick. She heard the dog move in dry leaves under the log lean-to. She felt the springs of the old armchair pierce her buttock through her roll-on.

'Now, Mr Bar-Lev, do you have fuel for the winter?' It was a few minutes before the old man succeeded in collecting his thoughts around fuel neatly enough to be able to reply that he had bought logs, and collected fallen branches himself. They were all stacked in the lean-to. He would show Miss Gluckstein.

'And how about stores? You remember last year you were cut off for ten days in all that dreadful snow . . .' There was another pause while Mr Bar-Lev made a concerted effort to focus on Miss Gluckstein's centres of interest. No, he admitted, he had not done anything about stores for the winter. But, yes, he would – next week. Definitely. Miss Gluckstein handed him a sheet of paper on which she had listed the provisions she thought essential: tinned food, candles, paraffin, etc.

'If you hand this to Mrs Lloyd, and ask her to get Dai to bring everything right up to the front door, I will see they are adequately reimbursed for the little extra service. Miss Gluckstein did so hope her plans would prove foolproof. Last year, she remembered, she had left it to Mr Bar-Lev himself to carry the boxes of stores from the road where Dai had left them for him. Mr Bar-Lev had forgotten the details of the arrangement and his dry goods had become sodden goods.

'Do you have mice?' Miss Gluckstein enquired, her gaze settling on a patch of the stone floor.

'I do!' replied Mr Bar-Lev, not without pleasure. Miss Gluckstein congratulated herself on the quality of her eyesight: those were not Caraway seeds. What would Mr Bar-Lev have been doing with spices? Certainly not cake-making.

'I don't think it healthy, you know – they carry disease.' Mr Bar-Lev agreed on both points, but what could he decently do? The little creatures came in out of the cold of the fields, and it would be appalling to repay their trust by setting traps. This topic of conversation was one which Miss Gluckstein had opened up before. She had quickly discovered that it only revealed Mr Bar-Lev's respect for *all* of God's creation, and did nothing to allay her abiding fear of germs. She made no progress.

'Are there any little practical matters I can attend to for you?' Miss Gluckstein asked in a kindly voice that did not reflect the feelings in her desiccated breast. The old man passed her a heavy sweater and indicated gaping holes where the elbows once had been. Miss Gluckstein dived into one of her zipped bags and found wool and a darning needle: it was not the first time she had been called upon to reinstate this garment. As she darned, Mr Bar-Lev clumsily set about fitting into his wireless the batteries Miss Gluckstein had brought him. Suddenly, words and music erupted into the silence of the cottage. The dog, startled, howled furiously outside.

'Shall we have that a little less loud, Mr Bar-Lev?' The old man's fingers fumbled with the control knobs.

THE RETURN

It would have been obvious to anyone observing Miss Gluckstein and Mr Bar-Lev under the same roof, she in the broken-down armchair, mending, he alternately staring out of the window and reading snatches of a journal, that this bear of a man and this mouse of a woman had something profound in common. Their behaviour was altogether habitual, their relationship a marriage of sorts (the only marriage Miss Gluckstein had known). Neither showed surprise: the questions posed, the answers given, both were in keeping with expectations. Their conversation, and the topics around which their conversation ambled, was formalized by a ritual each instinctively performed. It was because Miss Gluckstein had an *untried* matter to put to her client before she left for London that this particular visit was uneasy for her. In her mind all was ordered according to established rules, but there was no precedent for what she had to broach today. Mr Bar-Lev had always shown a reluctance to discuss his work and his life with her — and with other members of the JCR. Was it likely that he would agree to broadcast on both?

'May I have some light?' Miss Gluckstein asked, as she strained to see the neat wicker of her darning. Mr Bar-Lev moved an oil lamp across the table and lit it.

The sun was sinking between two folds of hills. The golden leaves of the beech tree outside the cottage window caught at its faint autumnal rays. With a flourish, Miss Gluckstein put down Mr Bar-Lev's woollen, thrust the darning needle into the ball of wool and put both into her bag. She said she must be preparing to 'make tracks' but, she added, just before she did so she had something to discuss with him. Her training — and her natural suspicion of the non-Jewish world — led her to be almost fanatically protective of her clients. The fact that she had to rely on the Lloyd family to facilitate her care of Mr Bar-Lev in no way contravened her predilection for secrecy: they were Welsh, they were villagers! Their knowledge of Mr Bar-Lev's financial situation could not possibly have unwelcome repercussions, for their world was cut off from the world of danger. But the BBC! Oxford! Another thing altogether.

'How is your work progressing?'

'Very well! Very well indeed!'

'Good!' But did that mean Mr Bar-Lev would be more or less likely to fall in with Miss Anders's request?

'I wonder whether you might be willing to take a few days off work to talk to a young lady about your early days in Paris?' This suggestion, being so remote from any familiar thought, seemed unanswerable to Mr Bar-Lev and so he ignored it. Undaunted, Miss Gluckstein elaborated. A Miss Auriol Anders, from the BBC, had telephoned her at the office to ask whether she knew the whereabouts of a Mr Bar-Lev whom she, Miss Anders, had met briefly at Oxford.

'I was very careful what I said, I can assure you. I know how much you value your privacy.'

'Miss Anderson! Who is this lady? I don't remember meeting a Miss Anderson!' Miss Gluckstein was hardly surprised that her client's memory failed him in matters relating to the real and actual world: it always did. She repeated.

'She was a student when you were a Fellow. She was a friend of Mr Vaughan. And her name is *Anders*...'

'Ah!' The light was dawning. 'Ah! Yes! Perhaps I do remember!' Mr Bar-Lev stood at the window, vaguely remembering. Oxford – spires, river, libraries – swam into his mind while Miss Gluckstein divided herself between preparations for her departure and attention to a studied nonchalance that would not arouse the old man's resistance.

'Did you tell her where I was living?'

'Of course not! I told her to write to me with details of the programme she was making and I would look into the matter.'

'What does she want to see *me* for?' The old man shuffled across the room and sat down with a thump on the arm of his chair.

'She didn't say too precisely. Just that she was looking for people who had known Proust personally. She told me she had been interested in the subject of your book, too.'

'The BBC interested in Jewish mysticism?' Mr Bar-Lev's voice rose incredulously. He had seen television when he had dropped in on Mrs Lloyd one Sunday, believing it to be Monday. A noisy box on wheels in the corner of the room, garnished with a potted plant, intrusive as a nagging child. He remembered the cat slept in front of it. And he had seen it at The Sheep's Bell. An extraordinary machine – it could get two rugger sides into its picture. Two rugger sides in about twelve inches. Mr Bar-Lev's mind got stuck into considerations of this kind, and would have lingered there longer had Miss Gluckstein not been in one of her hurries.

'I believe Miss Anders and others are making a series of programmes about Marcel Proust. It is the one-hundredth anniversary of his birth next July. There are not many people left who knew him, she told me. She is scouring the country. Was he such a great writer to deserve all this fuss?'

Inadvertently Miss Gluckstein had drawn together two threads of her client's life she had no reason to know were connected. Neither had any premonition that drawing together the two strands would be explosive.

'Ach! I haven't thought of Marcel for years! What a dear man!'

'May I give Miss Anders your address? I know she would like to come up here to talk to you.'

'Will she pay me?' Miss Gluckstein could not believe the evidence of her ears. No question her client could have put would have surprised her more. Mr Bar-Lev's relationship with money was at best casual. He seemed, in his daily life, to

WILL DOLORES COME TO TEA?

have very little idea of the connection between money and survival. Certainly, he had never shown the least interest in acquiring it. And now, on this momentous occasion, when he was quite suddenly to be drawn into the mainstream, he was asking about money. Miss Gluckstein was dumbfounded.

'I very much doubt that she will pay to come and talk to you!' she replied, a mite caustically, 'But if you appear on her television programme you are likely to be paid a good deal.'

Mr Bar-Lev considered the carrot that led to carrots.

'How much, do you suppose?'

'I'm afraid I can't tell you that. I just don't know. But it is always said that television pays very well indeed. You could ask Miss Anders when she comes to see you.' By now Miss Gluckstein was stationed at the cottage door. Mr Bar-Lev heaved himself off the arm of his chair and moved towards his table. He shuffled some papers and stood his passport against a dirty milk bottle.

'You may tell Miss Anderson I shall be delighted to see her,' he said.

The sound of a car horn in the valley alerted Miss Gluckstein. She lifted the latch quickly, but before opening the door she turned to Bar-Lev once more.

'Now please remember, you have said you will see Miss Anders. I shall pass your message on to her and she will be most upset if you forget, or go back on your word!' As Miss Gluckstein picked her way down the track, Mr Bar-Lev untied his dog and let him into the cottage. The old man was smiling. He sat down in the armchair with his dog sprawled across his feet, stretched over to the table and turned off the lamp. The only sound was that of wood crackling in the stove; the only light that of orange rays the setting sun was spilling on his floor. Mr Bar-Lev was at peace, and he slept.

∞

Auriol Anders took down the rather complicated instructions

Miss Gluckstein provided regarding Mr Bar-Lev's present whereabouts and how to contact him. It came as no surprise to Auriol to be confronted by complications; it was many years since she had seen Mr Bar-Lev but his eccentricities featured large in her memories of him. She wrote to him, care of the post office, Gwyn Conwen, and prepared herself for a long wait before he replied. She was not disappointed: her letter — and the one from Miss Gluckstein with his November cheque — remained uncollected for fifteen days while Bar-Lev, trapped in a thicket of research, struggled to extricate himself from a new and thorny problem, oblivious to his diminishing stores of food and paraffin. Eventually, Mrs Lloyd got Dai to call at the cottage with a note from her good self, saying his cheque had arrived and a letter.

'I wonder who it's from, Dai, I don't recognize the hand.'

Mr Bar-Lev was not at home when Dai called. He was on the mountain with Adler. He had gone, specifically, to sit on a felled stump by the dewpond at the summit, where the mountain peak, having suffered some geological sabotage, levelled to a treeless plateau. It was here the old man repaired when he had a particularly knotty problem to solve. In summer he was always surprised and delighted to find the rich carpet of *mille fiori* growing among the luxuriant pink grasses. And in winter, despite icy winds and snow, the dewpond was never frozen. But this was no ordinary place. It was hallowed. The silence on the plateau, at all seasons, gave rise to an articulacy to which Adler too responded. Bar-Lev felt on his pulse the vibration from the chord of ordered harmony God had inadvertently but mercifully introduced into the chaos of His creation.

It was five weeks before Bar-Lev returned the stamped and addressed envelope Miss Anders had thoughtfully enclosed with her letter. She had gone so far as to type a card: 'I will/will not be available on Friday, 27 November at about 2.30 p.m.' indicating Mr Bar-Lev should strike out what did not apply, and in the case of the date and time not being convenient that he should suggest alternatives.

Miss Gluckstein's instructions had covered every detail. Auriol Anders recognised the grass verge at the bottom of the track that led to Bar-Lev's cottage, and parked her car. The track that wound uphill was humped in the middle and worn and mud-filled at the edges. She listened, impressed by the silence made more profound by the chimes of the church clock striking two. She had eaten an undistinguished lunch at a pub in Builth Wells, since when more exacting subjects than that of the indifferent quality of pub food had been excluded from her mind. But as she got out of the car, into the silence of the sun-filled cold, and took two bags of provisions out of the boot, her thoughts turned to the man for whom she had driven some one hundred and fifty miles.

Adler had notified Bar-Lev of his visitor's approach and his bark had confirmed to Auriol that she was heading in the right direction. As she picked her way up the lane, her eyes fastened on the perils of the path, Bar-Lev had the advantage of her.

'I do recognize you!' he said warmly, as she approached. He was unashamedly delighted by the sight of his visitor. Auriol was thirty-eight: she had a wide, engaging smile and had arrived at that time in life when youth and experience combine and blend, rather than cancel one another out. And she was beautiful. With the word 'beautiful' forming in his mind details clustered round the image, whole passages of time, warm, pleasant, exciting. He wished he might persuade them to linger, to float in his consciousness like fragile birds on a gentle upstream of warm air: 'Joy wants itself eternally . . .'

'And of course I recognize you!' Auriol put down the bags she was carrying and surveyed the man, his cottage and the view over the valley. She held out her hand and the old man took it in his right hand and with his left drew her into the cottage. The provisions would have been forgotten in the lane had Adler not drawn attention to them by sniffing round them. Auriol retrieved them. The old man was in a state of nervous excitement, and was mumbling loudly. Auriol, although triumphant at having discovered him, was also overwhelmed by the dirt and disorder around him. The word 'neglect' was foremost in her mind. For a man of his age, surely his physical well-being was not being catered to. Mentally, he was obviously confused. She wondered how she would penetrate the chaos and sift from the dust the nuggets of precious material she was here to prospect. If the cottage, with its stacks of old papers, its broken-down furniture, its crumbling plaster and unwashed dishes, reflected Bar-Lev's state of being, she would be facing insuperable difficulties.

∞

Auriol was a compassionate woman and an experienced interviewer. Her intelligence and her perception had long been underemployed interviewing luminaries from the world of politics and other performing arts. She was inherently a dreamer, whose interests lay in corners from which television cameras were excluded. Her daydreaming was mistaken for apathy both by her bosses and her more ambitious female colleagues, whose perceptions were media-thin and whose upward mobility was thinly disguised. But men she met socially were attracted to this quality of other-worldliness, even if somewhat bemused by it: what are you thinking? they wanted to know. Their sixth sense led them to suppose it was not they or their well-being that detained her. But their admiration of her physical appearance, and the mystery her cool detachment created, stimulated the desire to colonize her, and overcame any slight her seeming indifference created. For interviewing Bar-Lev, Auriol's qualities were ideal and her beauty would stir memories in a man whose appreciation of the female form had had little upon which to feast these many years.

Bar-Lev seemed to Auriol older than his seventy-three or -four years, his body's parts only loosely adhering, his mind wandering. She felt most comfortable when the old man ceased tottering about the room between piles of papers and other oddments, and settled into his broken armchair. She judged that probably the distant past would be most readily accessible to recall, and for this reason she urged him: start at the beginning, right at the beginning.

'Where were you born?' For two days Bar-Lev spoke of Spoltz, the place and its inhabitants. He spoke of his father and his mother.

Auriol spent seven days in the company of Bar-Lev. On the very first she succeeded in prising open gates to the past through which, over the following six days, a stream of memories poured unimpeded. The old man was not disturbed by the tape recorder; if he registered its presence he did not register its function. Bar-Lev, characterized by a daunting intellectual and emotional honesty, including an unerring ability to distinguish the significant from the insignificant, would do nothing to censor his memories. He realized that much of what he said had been considered socially unacceptable sixty years before, but because these judgements had been made by ignorant and unfeeling men, he ignored such prejudices. His descriptions of the most intimate and exotic events were delivered without a hint of prurience.

∞

Lev Bar-Lev had been born in central Europe in an extended village then in Poland but throughout its history snatched by various conquering nations for its strategic geographic position. Like the Jews themselves the name of the place did not survive the physical onslaughts of Russians, Germans and

Poles, but in B-L's childhood the village had been called Spoltz.

'As I remember, the village was divided in two, both geographically and socially: the Polish-Christian quarter was a hell-hag, the Jewish ghetto my tutelary saint. But that distinction became less marked as I grew up. Because of my father's rejection of orthodoxy and his espousal of mysticism the distinctions became muddled and I became an exile in exile. But at least I lived to tell the tale.'

With Auriol's tactful encouragement B-L loosed the restraining bonds that normally contained his past. He described Polish-Christian Spoltz as a lonely, crumbling old woman of a place, physically ugly, dugs slung low, incontinent, hair a thatch where scavenger birds stored prey, eyes curtained by cataracts, breath foul and nose now clogged, now running with yellowish phlegm, her person never more than partially concealed under rags that neither kept out the weather nor the gaze she should not have solicited. In later years when he had found himself in the ports of North Africa and in the *barrancas* of Latin America, his nose assailed by the stench of human excrement and rotting vegetable waste and the festering innards of long-dead animals, he had immediately been transported to the market-place in Spoltz. That same stinking aroma had hung over the Polish quarter in a never-dispersing cloud, lurking in all its alleys, but bursting forth particularly boisterously upon the market-place, for there the gutters were always blocked with garbage picked over and scattered by vagrant dogs that only added to the filth. It was a strange fact, he recalled, that the market-place in Spoltz was such a threatening, unlovable memory, for his mother sold her wares there, and he had often accompanied her. But his mother seldom left him alone with her eggs, her vegetables, her pickles and preserves, and she laid down strict rules for the route he must follow home if he did not wait to return with her. He was forbidden the short cut through the narrow alley where strange men and women gathered and spilled their partly clad shadows. 'The devil's abode lies that way,' his mother warned.

There was a single road that led direct from the market-place to the ghetto. It was the road to Warsaw. But it was more than that, much more than that, for the Jews: it was the way OUT. Pedlars came from the direction of Warsaw and along with their wares sold tantalizing dreams. Poles drove down the Warsaw road in their carts, or walked from the market-place, but only as far as the fork: to the right the road made a circle round Spoltz, taking in the church and cemetery and the sugar-beet warehouse, before returning to the market-place; to the left, a little further on, stood the Jewish ritual slaughterhouse and bathhouse. The fork in the road stood as a permanent memorial of a singular kind. Here, at this junction, the Christian God and the Jewish God parted company. A few hundred yards further down the Warsaw road, beyond the slaughterhouse and bathhouse, stood the synagogue, and beyond it the one-storey wooden houses belonging to the Jews. When one of the richer Poles had business in Warsaw he did not take the Warsaw road past the Jewish houses, he made a detour to spare his Christian sensibilities. A lane that started at the church joined the Warsaw road a mile or two beyond the ghetto.

Bar-Lev took from a toppling pile of books by his chair an old atlas that had lost its covers, shuffled through its pages until he found the page he sought. He pointed out to Auriol a red circle drawn round a word in Cyrillic.

'You see, my dear! Insignificant in itself, but on the way to great places!' He laughed. Auriol saw that faded red lines led from what she assumed to be Spoltz, linking the village with Warsaw, Moscow, Paris and Berlin.

'Had my mother been as deaf to the resonances of the

greater world as the rest of the community, had my father been less imaginative, had the Jews of Spoltz been less bigoted, I would not be here. I too would be a flake of ash in the wind.' His eyelids fell closed against the thought.

'It seems impossible, yet I believe my mother and father led happy lives. Despite the threats that were posed daily from the very existence of the Poles on our heels, my parents and other Jews lived happily *because they lived religiously, in the absolute certainty of the mercy of their God.* It is hard for a non-Jew to understand the way in which Jews survive; it is a marvel of our psychology. We continuously expect to be wiped from the face of the earth at a moment's notice, but we also expect God to exact retribution from our aggressors, and lead us into a land flowing with milk and honey. The fact that we have been consistently wrong, so far as the latter is concerned, does nothing to lessen our faith. God makes mistakes! God takes his time! If the ways of God seem unfathomable to us it is only because He does not wish us to understand them thoroughly. But this doesn't mean that the covenant we made with him has been cancelled. Adherence to the Law provides full spiritual cover.

'My parents had seven or eight children, but by the time I was five my brothers were all at work and my sisters dead. Being the youngest by many years I was especially treasured, and I felt myself to be my parents' only child. Sixty-odd years on, when I dream of Spoltz, I am always alone with my parents. I see myself sitting with my father at his workbench, alone, or watching my mother prepare food in the kitchen, or selling her produce in the market, alone. Or I am with both my parents in the vegetable plot we shared with neighbours, pulling radishes and planting cabbages. I see us walking to the synagogue on the Sabbath, father in front of mother and me bringing up the rear. We are alone together – apart from the rest of the community.

'Until the tragedy that befell us we were wholly interdependent. I needed my parents' care and they needed to provide it. Our living conditions were very modest – this cottage for one man is spacious by comparison – but I loved that house in Spoltz. It was home.

'The houses in which we Jews lived were strung together and formed a number of squares. Each house faced on to a courtyard, which was communal, and backed on to the road. My mother could always see me from the kitchen window when I was playing in the yard. My father could keep an eye on me from his workshop; it too faced on to the yard. Until the tragedy, I was well protected.'

Bar-Lev recalled these details slowly, painfully. Between episodes he resumed his habitual mumbling, and he passed his hands over his face in the manner of a cat washing itself. When he moved in his old chair, it appeared to Auriol as if he were about to adopt the rocking motion peculiar to the mentally ill, but in fact he was moving to avoid the springs of the chair that drove into his backside. He had put up with the chair for so long that he did not register that his discomfort was caused by protruding springs; nevertheless he withdrew from their attentions at regular intervals. So long as he gave expression to the images that flooded his memory Bar-Lev found no difficulty in talking, but as soon as Auriol interrupted, to retrieve the old man's attention and fix it on the subject of her enquiry, he started mumbling. He was unused to sustained conversation, the batting to and fro of material from one human being to another. It was something he could do with his selves: with Bar-Lev the exiled child, Bar-Lev the scholar, Bar-Lev the friend and lover, Bar-Lev the hermit and believer, but interrogation by another came as a series of painful shocks. They were not the right questions; the questions were not being asked in sequence; the logic of his argument was being disregarded, undermined;

and misunderstanding heaped upon misunderstanding ... His anxieties only dissolved when he opened his eyes and saw before him the beautiful young woman. How could she understand? He excused her willingly. After all, was it not after nearly a lifetime that he himself was coming to some sort of understanding? It was as if from miles away, from under the ocean perhaps, that Bar-Lev heard Auriol's voice questioning.

'And what was the tragedy that befell?'

'My father went mad!' The sound of crackling wood made the silence behind those words a vehicle for their awesomeness. 'At least that was what everyone believed. He became "possessed". It happened in a split second, witnessed by me, by my mother, and by the whole Jewish community of Spoltz. It happened at midday in the heat of summer, in the market-place.' A tantalizing silence ensued. Auriol waited, conscious of the sound of her own heartbeat. 'It is a fact, of course, that any behaviour that departs from the norm is invariably regarded as mad or wrong — or both. The people here, in Gwyn Conwen, think I'm mad because I live alone and don't apply my memory to the things to which they apply theirs.' He stopped to consider what he had said and then almost barked: 'Of course, the danger of such judgements is even worse when you consider what they regard as *sane*...' Bar-Lev's tone had subtly modulated, and conveyed to Auriol an indignation of infinite proportions.

'My father's behaviour was anti-social — but he was far from mad. It was mysteriously revealed to him that he had been worshipping the wrong God, that the relationship he thought he had with his maker was an illusion. Like all converts to "the truth" his apostasy was dramatic.' Auriol found Bar-Lev's intensity frightening.

The old man got up and shuffled to the kettle. 'I shall make you tea,' he announced as if aware of the need to defuse something in the situation. 'So, you are interested in Marcel Proust, are you not? He too was horribly misjudged!' He shook his head in a gesture of disbelief. 'I don't say anyone has suggested he was actually *insane*, but his biographers have all made much of the fact that he was perverse, which they regard as worse, since it entails choice – and he made the wrong one. They portray Marcel as morally disabled. Poor darling, like most great men he has had to endure being interpreted by inferior mortals, men without imagination, men who in most cases don't even do their research conscientiously.'

Auriol judged the moment propitious for her first direct question regarding Proust. Bar-Lev was undoubtedly pondering Proust's moral probity, and before his thoughts settled elsewhere she must excavate where the ground seemed friable.

'Tell me, did Marcel Proust *found* a male brothel? Or did he simply frequent such places?'

'Yes to both your questions.' But here Bar-Lev paused for what seemed to Auriol a long time. 'The events are well known. Indeed, when I first met Marcel in 1917, he had just lent Albert le Cuziat the money to buy the lease on the Hôtel Marigny, and provided him with the tables, chairs, sofas, rugs and other bits and pieces that had been left to him by his parents. But, and this is a very significant "but", it is not true that he was, in the ordinary way, a client of Albert's establishment – or any other establishments.' Bar-Lev was excited, he was indignant. 'It is much more complicated than that. Marcel approved the formation of a centre of degradation and transgression – he understood its worth – and for his own purposes he needed a safe house. In return for the loan he made Albert, Albert provided him with rooms where he would not be disturbed. The holy sinner requires the sanctified to defile: Marcel hid behind the shuttered windows of a male brothel tricked out in his family heirlooms, knowing that only a very obvious conclusion would be drawn by gossips, and the real purpose of his visits would not come to light.'

'The "real purpose"?'

'An English biographer of Marcel has written that at this time Marcel was "experimenting with evil", "testing his power to associate with it unscathed". It is remarkable – quite fascinating – how near the biographer got to a truth of which he himself was unaware. Perhaps he intuited something he failed to bring to the surface of his mind . . . But I'm tired now. Let this wait until tomorrow.'

Bar-Lev was more alert the next morning than Auriol had seen him. The sluice gates had been opened and he was anxious, now he had organized what he was going to talk about, to get started. He was making tea when Auriol arrived. She dispensed with pleasantries, and accepted the tea in which the old man had put a spoonful of jam. She had hardly turned on the tape recorder before Bar-Lev spoke. 'You know that I've spent my whole adult working life on Sabbatai Sevi – true, I've had to publish other things along the way but Sevi has been my real work. I embarked on this study of him because my dear father believed himself to be the reincarnation of Sevi, the Holy Sinner. Everything that has happened to me since my father revealed this to us in Spoltz owes itself to that revelation. First, because of the problems my father's divided self created, my mother sent me to live with relatives in Paris – a terrible trauma, a terrible sadness for me. But that's another story and we haven't time for it. Secondly, I happened upon Marcel Proust and his friend Chaim Saul-Dubrovsky, and their little group of Sabbatians. My exile only found its meaning when I entered Marcel's rooms at the Hôtel Marigny, and the shape of my life since has followed the contours of my study of Sevi.'

'Proust! A Sabbatian!' Auriol showed astonishment and

by so doing staunched the flow of Bar-Lev's words. There was a note of disbelief in her exclamation – even distaste. The old man rose and went to the window and looked out. 'If you will forgive me I think I would rather stop our talk for today. I have agreed to answer your questions and I shall honour that agreement. But now the time has come for me to describe the events that led to my exile. They are distressing to recall; I prefer to think of them in short snatches only. I hope to feel more able tomorrow. So, if you will excuse me, my dear.' Bar-Lev made it clear to Auriol he would like her to go.

Auriol left the cottage feeling deeply depressed. First, she should not have shown shock over Proust. Secondly, there was something distasteful in evoking in an old man memories so painful that he must have had to bury them in order to survive. It crossed her mind that the obligation he felt to reveal himself to her might kill him.

༄

'It was summer. I remember the season because Mother had bunches of fresh dill on top of the egg basket, and because there was newly-made plum jam and raspberry cordial to sell. I can see them now, as I speak, arranged on the upturned boxes in the market-place. Mother had me sit behind the boxes and watch over the produce while she moved a few yards to the right or left to speak to a neighbour or friend. "Don't you take your eyes off the produce, my son!" she would warn, believing the whole market alive with jam and cordial thieves. But she never ventured far; she always kept me within sight, so that on the day on which my life was shattered my mother was only a few yards away.

'I don't remember what struck me first – the sight of my father or the commotion, but all of a sudden the market-place was stilled. With shock. My father was running through the narrow alleys between the stalls, naked! Boys and girls of my age and older pursued him. They were Polish girls and boys and they had rush wands in their hands and were beating Father. "Snip-cock! Snip-cock!" they shouted. I saw Mother look up and grow pale. She tore the shawl from her shoulders and raced towards father. As she ran she shouted to me to take care of the produce. I saw her catch up with Father and wind her shawl around his loins. I was shaking. But my main worry was how I would get the eggs home without breaking them. And then, as if conscious of my fear, a kindly neighbour came and bought the eggs and the herbs and gave me coins for them. I folded the coins in my handkerchief, as Mother had taught me to do. I put the unsold cordials and jams into the basket and I hauled them home. I can remember now the strange mixed feelings I had of fear and of importance in my new responsibility. All around me the Jews were discussing Father and how he had gone mad and would have to be sent away or locked up. "There are lunatics and lunatics," they said, "and such a lunatic we can't endure." But at the same time these people remembered who my father was — a craftsman, not such an important person in the community as a businessman, of course, but an honest man who was liked and had the reputation of being observant and wise. People came to him not only for their tables and their chairs and, finally, for their coffins, they came to him for his advice. His extraordinary behaviour that day was felt as a betrayal of their confidence in him, and it was this, perhaps, that made them so harsh.

'When I arrived home Father and Mother were seated at the table drinking tea with jam in it, as if it were any ordinary afternoon. I didn't like to ask what Father had been doing, and neither he nor Mother offered an explanation. I took the coins from my handkerchief and gave them to Mother, and she peered into the basket and found the remaining jams and cordials were sound. "You're a good boy Lev," she said, "a boy to be proud of!" And I remember being proud. I looked closely at Mother and Father, to see whether I could detect changes in them, but they seemed just the same. I think I felt secure enough to go out and play. But I know from that time I was perpetually anxious that someone would come and take Father away and lock him up. I asked Mother: "Will Father have to go away?" And I remember she told me, very softly, so he could not hear: "Of course not, my son, don't worry your head. Father was swimming in the stream and some naughty boys – may they perish – took his clothes..." And I was reassured. It did not occur to me at the time that Father would never swim in the stream, as we children did, and that had boys taken his clothes he would nevertheless not have needed to run naked through the marketplace to return home and clothe himself.

'And then Father started to use language I didn't understand, and Mother would say: "Please! Not in front of the child." Once he came home from a walk saying it had been raining carp. I laughed and laughed. "Mother, Mother, Father was caught in a carp storm!" I called out. But Father was not laughing. "Where I walk anything can happen!" he announced solemnly. I took his cue, and ceased laughing. I was inclined to believe him, I was so proud of him. "Don't stuff the boy's head with your nonsense!" Mother urged, gently but firmly. Then I started to notice other things.

'Father ceased to wear at his waist the girdle that divides the sacred part of the body from the profane. Several times, when I found the girdle lying on the floor or stuffed into a cupboard, I would run after him reminding him of what he had forgotten. One day I watched in horror as he set light to it; eventually he burnt it to ashes in the yard on kindling that seemed to crackle with delight as it consumed the sacred barrier. I was terrified. I ran into the kitchen and told Mother who, with her hands and arms white with flour, ran into the yard crying, "What *will* the neighbours say!" Then it was, perhaps for the first time in my life, I heard my mother and father screaming at one another. How I wept! I knew that something of enormous proportions was happening, and that everything was at stake. I expected to see Father burn the house down next; I expected to see Mother rend her garments and weep for all eternity. I felt the end of our world was nigh. I was a child of ten years and understood so little about that girdle and yet I knew, knew at some deep level, its immense significance, and knew that to destroy it meant the destruction of family life.

'Father walked through the house, picked up one or two objects – I don't remember what – and left, slamming the door. Mother stayed weeping at the kitchen table. I buried my head in her lap, and clung to her. I wet my pants.

'Other events took place. One day when Mother was at market I was at home with a fever. Mother had wrapped me in her quilt and put me in her bed and told me if I wanted anything I was to ring a little handbell she put beside me and Father would hear in the workshop and come and see what I wanted. I slept on and off, and towards noon, when Father would normally have gone to the kitchen to make himself something to eat, I woke to find him by the bed dressed in Mother's Sabbath dress. He smiled the oddest smile at me. I slipped back into sleep. When I told Mother: "Father put on your Sabbath dress!" she said soothingly, "You have a bad fever, my son. Fever makes for strange dreams."

'But it was not the case that my fever had produced that sight and when I was well again I saw Father in the street, once again dressed in Mother's Sabbath dress, this time swinging her rope of pearls, with her Sabbath wig at an angle on his head. He aped the manner of women and minced along the unmade road, singing a high-pitched song. I ran behind a shed. I watched, terrified: terrified lest anyone else should see him. And then I ran ahead of Father and turned back to face him and begged him, "Come home, Father! Come home! They will see you. All the neighbours, they will see you!" I can remember the expression on his face, even today. It was peculiar, so peculiar I only half-recognized my own father, and this frightened me horribly. I kept on pushing him, trying to get him to go back homewards. The feel of silky material under my fingers, clothing my father, felt revolting. All the time I was warning him that people would see him. I did not like to push him too hard, for fear of pushing him right over. I was crying. And I didn't succeed in stopping him. He continued to walk in the direction of the synagogue. I ran off back home and as I ran I could see little groups of our neighbours gathering, pointing at Father and laughing. One or two boys of my age, boys I knew, picked up stones and threw them at Father. But when they saw him lift up Mother's skirts and relieve himself by the roadside they were so shocked they held their fire.

'One of the most humiliating things he was doing was exposing himself all over Spoltz. One day, when the rabbi called at the house, I thought he must be coming to reprimand Father about that. Father ushered the rabbi into the bedroom for the sake of privacy but the walls were paper-thin. I sat at the kitchen table and heard every word.

'"I am in love with your wife!" Father was confiding to the rabbi, "and she with me. We lie together when your back is turned. You are an ignorant, silly little man. When we lie together we spit on your prayer-book and take your Sabbath *talis* to wipe our loins." Those words stuck in my mind because it was so astonishing for anyone to address the rabbi without respect. To call him "ignorant" was, perhaps, the worst of all. My mother had slipped into the kitchen from the yard and was listening with me. To catch every word she moved to the bedroom door and applied her ear to it. Then she swooned. When Father opened the door and thrust the rabbi out into the kitchen he almost fell over Mother, who lay sprawled at his feet.

'Mother had been humiliated beyond endurance. In addition to all she had heard from Father's lips, she had heard the rabbi say that the synagogue was now closed to Father. There was nothing more terrible for Mother than to be married to a man excluded from his place of worship. I think it was as much that as his professed infidelity that made her swoon. I fetched water for her and held the cup to her lips as she drank. Father stood to one side, watching. As soon as Mother appeared to have come round Father approached her, but she screamed and tried to evade him by crawling on all fours into the cupboard. I remember the feeling of icy cold that came over me as I watched Mother grapple with the door to the cupboard and heard it slam behind her. From outside the closed cupboard door Father addressed her in words which seemed to come from the realm of the prayer-book: "My beloved wife, you must understand that if I eat pork, piss in the market-place, expose my sex to the neighbours and lie with the rabbi's wife, it is not because I so desire but because duty impels me so to do. If, God forbid, our beloved son Lev should stumble into the well in the potato field, would not you or I descend as deep as was required to rescue him? Of course we would. It is such a descent that I am making. The sparks of goodness that Almighty God mislaid are sunk deep in the bowels of human experience. I am obliged to filthy myself because it is my task to retrieve them. My next step is to convert to Christianity – and take Lev with me. He will shortly be baptised!" I remember my father's words so clearly because when Mother heard that Father intended to have me baptised she exploded from the cupboard, wrapped me in her arms and ran, faster than she or I knew she was able, to the *shammas*, and he wrote down what Father had said, intending to give a verbatim report to the rabbi. Mother repeated the words to herself as if they were some sort of litany and they have been engraved on my memory ever since. They have an awesome power about them, don't they?

'From that day Mother followed a routine of behaviour normally reserved for the days following a death in the family: she covered the mirror in the kitchen, she strewed the floor with straw, she rent her dress, she shrouded the candelabrum with a tablecloth and took a low stool out of the workshop to sit on. She appeared to be in a trance. Back and forth she swayed on the stool, moaning: "Dead to me! Dead to you and me! Dead!"

'"Their good opinion is of no concern to me," Father told Mother when she ceased swaying long enough to tell Father that the neighbours would no longer come for their chairs and their tables, their cupboards and their coffins – let alone advice – from a carpenter who was not only mad but bad. And we would starve.

'"They may laugh at me. They may scorn me. Let them! But look at them! Do you imagine it will be those God-fearing Jews of Spoltz who will bring our souls to the foot of the Throne of Glory? Mark my words: it won't be them! I who lust, fornicate, degrade myself in pursuit of the Divine: it is I who shall set you all free. In my degeneracy I have found a spark brighter than all others: with it between my teeth I can cleanse my defamed mouth, rinse my saliva in the waters of Eden and feel the liquid pass through my body right down to its basest places. Meanwhile my soul shall journey to the celestial places. There, where all is sharp, clear and bright, ringing with the chimes of righteousness, fragrant as the fields of roses of Sharon and lilies of the valley, I shall luxuriate. But to win this eternal bliss I must first sink into the ordure of this world. Here! Now! I must risk flesh and spirit.

The spirit of Sabbatai Sevi is within me, directing me. The rabbis must stop to ponder the holy exhortation: 'Just as a grain of wheat must rot in the earth before it can sprout, so the deeds of the believers must be truly rotten before they can germinate the redemption.'" It was not until I met Marcel that I fully understood that Father's madness was of a holy kind.

'Mother's place at market was taken by another woman. No one came to Father for their carpentry; indeed, they crossed over to walk on the other side of the road if they spotted him a hundred yards away. The children were forbidden to play with me. The other children, the Poles, taunted me at first and eventually took to torturing me. We became penniless and no one would help Mother out.

'The pockets of Father's gaberdine were permanently stuffed with bundles of obscene writing, stories that circulated only among the Polish men. I saw Mother grab them and set light to them but there were always more: "Sevi always carried dirt into the synagogue!" Father would explain. "But you are denied the synagogue!" Mother reminded him as she watched the papers burn.

'I remember that things were sometimes better and sometimes worse; sometimes Father seemed to regain his old self, sometimes with a changed voice, changed gait, he was Sevi, soiling the sanctity of our family life. During one of his calmer periods he persuaded Mother to remove the low stool and all other evidence of the mourning she was observing for her marriage, and I remember she appeared to understand for a while that Father was not humiliating her for his own sake, but that he was undergoing some spiritual upheaval she was unequipped to comprehend. I say this because I remember that, even after the onset of Father's so-called madness, Mother continued for a while to keep that part of the Sabbath that is the woman's domain.

'I should perhaps explain to you the awesome significance of the Sabbath in the ghetto. It was not simply the seventh day of the week on which no one worked. It was a day quite unlike the other six days, in every smallest detail. It was a gift from God. It was the day to which we looked forward from the moment the sun set upon the Sabbath we had just celebrated. It was the day that made the other days tolerable. Even when there was not quite enough to eat, and no money for new boots, and the roof obstinately let in rain whatever precaution Father took, it didn't matter. If business was bad and if health was indifferent none the less the Sabbath would emerge from the shadows of the week and for twenty-four hours we would savour perfection. For such a glorious occasion, you can imagine, we prepared carefully. It was as if we were expecting the most hallowed guest. Perhaps that does best describe it, for the Sabbath was a bride in Spoltz: pure and joyful. The Sabbath provided a glimpse of the eternal world, the land of milk and honey, all that a bride promises her husband.

'In preparation for the Sabbath Mother cleaned out the house every Friday. She would start with the beds, stripping them down to their springs – and even washing the springs. She remade the beds with fresh linen, albeit patched but always smelling of bay. She piled the furniture into a castle in the middle of the kitchen and took her dusters and her besom into every corner. She scrubbed the table and chairs. She even removed everything from the cupboards, all the packets and bottles and jars, and wiped them and scrubbed the shelves before putting them back in place. She took our few clothes out of the long cupboard and shook them in the yard, and brushed them down. This ritual cleansing was quite as important to Mother as the recital of her prayers. She got very hot and tired on Fridays – there was the Sabbath cooking to be done as well as the cleaning – but she wore a smile on her face from daybreak: "It is my privilege to prepare for the Sabbath," she would say. And she timed her chores to finish just before the *shammas* came walking down our street, clanging his bell, crying out: "Jews to the bathhouse!" Then Mother gathered up a bundle of clean clothes, Sabbath clothes, and slipped out of the house to ritually cleanse every detail of her person.

'The observant Jew believes that on the Sabbath, if he adheres to the Law in every detail, his soul is joined by another, purer soul that has been lodging in the bosom of the Almighty during the six ordinary days of the week. While that pure soul is in his company nothing can spoil his joy: he gets a taste of the world to come, a taste that only on the Sabbath are his senses tuned to convey. The Law provides to make the Sabbath so clean, so good, so joyful, so congenial that the Jew is able to conjure up a picture of eternity from it: "A different world! No worry, no work." Bliss that comes from being replete.

'But then, quite suddenly, one late Friday afternoon as the *shammas* walked down our street, ringing his bell, Father barred Mother's way and would not let her leave the house for the ritual bath. He had that day forbidden her to bake the Sabbath loaf and warned her she would not be permitted to light the Sabbath candles. And in contravention of the good manners demanded by the Sabbath he cackled like a maniac, *not* remembering (as is especially required on the seventh day) the destruction of the Temple. I can hear that cackle even today; I can see Mother cover her eyes and pray, despite her deprivations, and I can remember knowing that however sincere her prayers she must now be without hope for the future. The rules she had learned to follow were as inflexible as the rising and setting of the sun; failing to observe them meant she could expect no mercy from God.

'Mother turned to Father and pleaded with him, asking

him why he spoke to her in such a manner, why he was denying her her observances. "Am I not keeping your house clean? Do I not keep the dietary laws; have you ever seen me mix milk and meat dishes or put a dirty cloth on the Sabbath table? Are you suddenly made sick by the food I prepare for you? Am I unable to locate the things you lose in the house? Am I no longer your queen on the Sabbath because I am grown old?" She took him through the long list of duties a Jewish husband would expect from his Jewish wife, things that, had she neglected them, might have become a source of grievance against her. Her voice became quiet, her sobs became loud. All Father said, over and over again, was "I am Sevi!"

'Not only did Father destroy the practices of their marriage but he threw into the fire the objects, the few objects Mother loved: her prayer-book, the book of Jewish legends from which she read to me, the case she had embroidered as a wedding gift for Father to keep his sacred *talis* in. She had to watch as, instead of making a libation over the wine, Father got drunk. There were no more blessings in our house. Father ceased to bless the day, our food – even God himself. He substituted curses, in words the meaning of which I did not understand, words which drew first tears, then supplication and finally sobs from Mother.

'One or two of the very poor of our community who had suffered untold misery and deprivation listened to Father and were tempted to follow his example. For them salvation did not appear likely through the orthodox channels they had been brought up to follow. But the rabbi got wind of the possible defection and bought their adherence to his rule with charity – a few garments and some food. The ghetto of Spoltz was stiff with fear and joined to despise Father. He had nothing to do but spend his time with me. He told me God was giving him control of the natural world as a sign of his authority. "We are so poor, my boy, would it not be a fine thing if the fish in the lake grew to an immense size and the trees in the orchard bore larger and more fruit? Then we should all be better fed. I shall walk out into the orchard and command the apples to swell; I shall go down to the lake and address the carp." Off he would strut, alone, returning to insist that in response to his commands the fruit had indeed increased in size and number and the fish likewise – both swelled to the size and shape of Sabbath loaves. "It is only a matter of time before my name will appear with that of God in a fiery column stretching from the market-place up into the heavens. Men will faint with terror as they look to the sky and see the moon shining white by day and the sun shining red by night. They will hide their heads under their coats as the stars fall from the heavens. They will block their ears as the sound of the raging tide sweeping over the sands, through the fields, drowning the cities and covering the hills, approaches Spoltz. Stay alert, I tell you. You will live to see my name proclaimed. You may despise me today. You may send me forth tomorrow. I may suffer torture in the future. Yes, I expect to suffer because I am recognized by man and sanctified by God. Watch! I shall start my healing work today. Bring me your lepers, your epileptics, your deformed, your dying...!" Father would take off down the street towards the centre of Spoltz, his arms outstretched, his mouth foaming.

'I half-believed and half-disbelieved Father and his powers. Would the merciful God, to whom we had been praying since the time of our exile, wish us to live in such penury and danger? Father knew of another God. It was this other God to whom he prayed, who answered Father. Strange things *were* happening in Spoltz; I knew of them; Father said they were signs. One of the scrolls of the Ark had burst into spontaneous combustion, for example, and one Sabbath the bench that ran along the east wall of the synagogue collapsed just when the men had stopped praying and turned to sit down on it, and so they landed on their backsides. The women in the gallery saw this and tittered. Such an occurrence was regarded as a sign, and all knew no good would come of it.

'Whenever something strange happened in Spoltz – and it was always something dreadful – "Bar-Lev the madman" was blamed for it. Mother realized that, denied the prospect of bliss in the eternal world by the God to whom she had entrusted herself, she must spare me such humiliations and eventual damnation as she controlled. Her maternal duty was, she believed, to send me out of Spoltz. No doubt separation was as terrible for her to contemplate as it was for me to endure. But exile is our condition; we Jews are accustomed to it and there is no shame in it. After all, we are all exiles until we gain the promised land. Father had created spiritual death for his family by insisting that the God we had been worshipping, whose laws we had been assiduously keeping, was the wrong, powerless God. Certainly, the fact that He had permitted such terrible things to befall us made Mother question His authenticity, and as she anxiously questioned so she became disorientated. The only certainty upon which she could fasten was that I should be sent away, as far away as it was possible to go.

'As I look back I see that Spoltz was not only a place but a condition. Had we been secure, Father's holy possession would not have posed the threat it did. We Jews were hovering between the destruction of the past, the desperate need to find meaning in the present, and the threat of destruction in the future. Our people were all sickly, harassed and poor; our Polish neighbours were not so sickly, harassed and poor. God may have given us the Law but was that enough, people were asking? The Messiah of the Christians had also been a carpenter... The community hovered between a feeling of revulsion towards Father and some sense of disappointment in God. They had gone through a lot on the road to their salvation – had the time not come for their deliverance? They were torn.

'Leaving Mother was pain such as I could not have imagined. I had never experienced anything like it, nothing as deep and sharp and unremitting. Even in the darkest days of my life as an adult I have never suffered as deeply since. Mother was a righteous woman, a woman of warmth and humanity, of humour and intelligence. She represented the world as it could be in its most generous form. When I rode out of Spoltz, dazed in misery, I knew my mother's seat in heaven was assured – but I feared for her place on earth. Although I did not trust the judgement of the rabbis, or that of the Poles, I knew that it would not be Father who redeemed the world; Mother, in her daily behaviour, was our greatest hope. She towered above the common clay. And it was she, Mother, who was sending me away, away into exile – rejecting me for good. Was I not worthy of her? Of course, she was doing this for my good, but how could my good be achieved apart from her?

'The jolting cart lumbered down the Warsaw road between the burgeoning crops. A big-bellied cow complained in its byre. I was leaving behind the scents of horses and cow-dung and milk straight from the udder. I caught sight of the water carrier – as usual he was losing water from the buckets that swung freely from his yoke. I watched as six peasants tried to pull a vast rake across a field that had been allowed to lie fallow too long. The peasants were hot and irritable, the land unyielding; only the wind would race unimpeded across that field of thistles, docks and stones. I gazed at the hedges, imprinting on my mind the sight of frail wild roses hung about in a froth of wild clematis. Beyond, a boy in the rye was swinging a cracker against the rooks. I thought: I must remember this.

'Trying hard not to weep, I thought about the food Mother prepared, especially the food we ate on the Sabbath. There was the dish of cinnamon-flavoured noodles in milk that was my favourite. Would I ever taste it again? Would Mother keep her promise and come and visit me? Paris was a long way away. I was to live with Aunt Selly and Uncle Hirsh. Mother said I would love them as if they were my parents. They were just like her and Father, only Uncle Hirsh knew who he was: himself alone. And the people in Paris, the Christians, were not as uncouth as the Poles, Mother told me. But there were more of them, she added darkly.

'That was the last I saw of my mother and father. I was ten years old. Since the day I was sent out of Spoltz no twenty-four hours have passed without my thinking about Mother and Father. My work is my memorial to them.'

∽

Auriol Anders had just two days left in which to plumb the depths of Proust's Sabbatianism. Bar-Lev was at pains to reassure her that whereas his father had been possessed by Sevi, and had imagined himself the Messiah with an obligation to save the entire Jewish people, Marcel regarded himself merely as a servant of the forthcoming Messiah, with a duty to pursue degradation in the service of love. Since love's expression included sexual expression, and because his relationship with his beloved *Maman* had not been, as it should have been, frank to the last detail, it was in the direction of sex that his Sabbatianism pointed. At last Marcel was able to combine his beloved with his real self, and in so doing enable her soul to regain its proper place of exaltation in the Godhead.

Auriol was relieved to learn that although Proust had been intent upon the rescue and redemption of the soul of his mother it had not involved him in the excesses to which

Bar-Lev's father had subjected himself.

'Are you still convinced of his sincerity?' she asked.

'Indeed I am! Marcel believed with certitude and passion. It did not cross my mind he had any ulterior motive. Nor did I ever question his practices. Those who did and who do are people whose morality is located in the groin. I have no time for such people, never had! If you think about it, what harm did Marcel do? A few rats that would otherwise have been killed with poison were stuck with hat pins. A few boys who, had they fallen into the clutches of evil men might have been drugged or even killed and certainly diseased lent themselves and their bodies in the execration of *Maman* to an otherwise kind, generous and sensitive man. I, watching, learned much and hoped to inform many.

'Marcel was a man without prejudice and having no prejudices he came to experience – whether religious, aesthetic or emotional – naked as a child. He was an innocent; he proceeded from a position of love and awakened love in all who met him. I regard him as profoundly religious: his faith was absolute, his generosity to the poor unfailing, and his succour of the sick unflagging. What more can a man offer to his fellows – and to God. I never knew a better man.'

Auriol listened intently as Bar-Lev spoke of the Marcel Proust he had known. It was not the man about whom the biographies were written, nor was it the man about whom the fashionable, who did not read his work but picked about in his pages and talked as if they knew his thought, nodded their heads in moral indignation. When Auriol finally left Bar-Lev she felt herself somehow different from the person who had come to Gwyn Conwen a week ago. She had gone through the disorientation that is a prerequisite of new perceptions.

When Bar-Lev found himself alone again he slipped back into his work and gloried in the quiet of the hills.

∞

WILL DOLORES COME TO TEA?

Dai called in at the cottage and warned Mr Bar-Lev that tomorrow he would be collecting him, driving him to Monmouth and putting him on the London train. Dai had brought along a letter and insisted the old man read it in his presence. The letter was from Miss Gluckstein and was filled with instructions, matters that quickly bored Bar-Lev: what to pack, where to leave his key, how to destroy all perishables, and so on and so forth.

'Mother and I will take care of Adler,' Dai told him.

'You are so good to me Dai, you and your mother. Do I ever thank you?'

'Oh yes! In your way,' the young man assured him. Next morning when Dai arrived at the bottom of the lane and sounded his horn Mr Bar-Lev was ready waiting for him, his case packed and secured with washing line, Adler on his lead, the front door locked, the rubbish burnt, and the key in a flower-pot in the log shed.

∞

Miss Gluckstein felt cold. She had arrived in good time for the train from Monmouth, anxious not to miss Mr Bar-Lev, only to discover the train would be late. Why was it, she wondered, that trains were invariably late and railway stations invariably cold — even in summer. What a good thing she had worn her brown outfit: British railway stations were dirty places. She felt a need, but she was certainly not going to satisfy it in the toilets on Paddington Station. She looked about her for a bench on which to sit. There was none free. She could go and have a cup of tea, she supposed, but what if she missed Mr Bar-Lev? It would be best to hang around the exit from Platform 8, she decided.

In her closely zipped bag she had Mr Bar-Lev's money and tickets. She had arranged with Auriol Anders that Mr Bar-Lev's fee for the various interviews he had agreed to give would be paid to her so that she could make the necessary arrangements. Unable to convince the BBC to pay out money before they had received the goods, Miss Anders herself had provided the advance out of her own pocket. Miss Gluckstein had had no difficulty organising Mr Bar-Lev's visa: a number of Jews were visiting Poland each year, and she had dealt with the Polish Embassy on their behalf half a dozen times. However, the thought of Mr Bar-Lev making such a long and emotional journey worried Miss Gluckstein. She was perfectly sure no good could come of it.

Bar-Lev shuffled towards her. His ancient leather suitcase, secured with the piece of washing-line cord, attracted her eye and her disapproval.

'My guardian angel!' Mr Bar-Lev dropped his suitcase and shook Miss Gluckstein's hand. It took much longer for Miss Gluckstein and her charge to cross the forecourt and hail a taxi than it took other travellers. Mr Bar-Lev was dazed and tired, Miss Gluckstein anxious and cold.

'I have booked you into a hotel between my office and my flat,' she told him. But he was not listening; he was staring out of the taxi window, stunned. 'I have arranged your appointments. The little film and the talks you have prepared are to be pre-recorded – except for just the one, on the tenth. And I've got your papers, your tickets and your money.' The word 'money' woke the old man from his preoccupations.

'You have my money! Good! Good!'

'Will you stay the whole month in Poland?'

'I can't say, Miss Gluckstein. But you are not to worry; you got me a return ticket. Trust me. I shall be back to give you all the inconvenience you are accustomed to from me!' And the old man laughed.

Miss Gluckstein insisted upon settling Mr Bar-Lev into his hotel room. She had an ulterior motive: she wanted to see for herself that he was dressed appropriately for his interviews. It came as no surprise to her that he was not.

'I shall pop round to Marks & Spencer,' she told him, 'and buy you a light jacket.' She decided not to buy him trousers because they would not be seen on television; in any case she did not know quite how to assess the size he would require. Mr Bar-Lev wore trousers that hung round his frame but did not touch his person except at the waist, where they were kept in place by anything that came to hand: string, cord, belt – one never knew. She agonized over his face: somehow he never quite succeeded in a proper shave. Perhaps he did not see clearly. Hairs sprouted from his ears and nostrils. Mr Bar-Lev did not smell too good, either, Miss Gluckstein discerned.

'Here's the bathroom. Plenty of hot water! That should be a nice change for you, Mr Bar-Lev, you can take as many baths as you like! It's all included in the price of the room.' Miss Gluckstein watched to see whether her words were making any impact. It was impossible to tell. 'Is there anything else I can get you at the shops?' she asked. Mr Bar-Lev turned and said yes, there was, 'Would you be so kind as to buy a large bunch of flowers for me to take to Miss Anders!' Miss Gluckstein sniffed: it was the 'large' that particularly affronted her. 'Here, take this!' The old man pulled a five-pound note from his pocket.

Miss Gluckstein left the inappropriately named Hotel Splendid and boarded a bus. She was rattled. Mr Bar-Lev was just as much trouble in London as he was up his Welsh mountain. Miss Anders was treating him like a celebrity; the members of the JCR were certainly not going to do likewise. All this running to and fro for this old man who was perfectly healthy and should be able to do the running for himself ... And there was the entire population of the Cohen Ward of the Jewish Hospital for the Terminally Ill waiting for her visit ...

Her mission accomplished, Miss Gluckstein returned to

the Hotel Splendid with a 'very suitable' jacket and a bunch of gladioli. Mr Bar-Lev was indifferent to both. They had the same effect upon him as his hotel room, the noise of the traffic and the smell of petrol and soot. Miss Gluckstein insisted he try on the jacket for size, and as he struggled out of his worn sweater and into the undistinguished garment she had selected she unconsciously sensed she had her client at a disadvantage: 'Has it been worth all these years of poverty and loneliness to write about that dreadful Sevi?' she asked.

'I've not been lonely, Miss Gluckstein. And see how far from impoverished I am when I have you to buy me clothes and food...' Then the mumbling started up, and Miss Gluckstein knew it was not worth pursuing the subject. Yet against her better judgement, she insisted, 'Why Sevi? He was an impostor. A man rejected by all decent Jews then and still rejected by us today.'

'So too was Jesus, Miss Gluckstein.' There was a pause during which Miss Gluckstein knew she was up to her ankles in a confrontation she was determined not to get up to her knees in. She did not know (and thank God for it!) a single other Jew who would bring up the name of Jesus in this or in any other context. Next thing he would be calling him 'Christ'.

'It was because he was rejected by so many Jews that I became interested in him. Being rejected by the majority is a reliable sign of worth.'

'If you ask me you might have done a greater service to your community if you'd studied Maimonides or the prophets.'

'There are always plenty of good Jews in the world, Miss Gluckstein, ready to do just that.'

Miss Gluckstein sniffed and drew on her beige fabric gloves which, she observed attentively, were not as clean as they had been when she left home. 'I'm going to take you over to Lime Grove now. Miss Anders is waiting with her other guests to see you.'

I do hope I shan't bump into Lady Cohen today, thought Miss Gluckstein as she stood in Southampton Row with Mr Bar-Lev, willing a taxi to appear quickly. Lady Cohen would certainly not approve the spectacle of Miss Gluckstein shepherding a dirty old man across London and might adjust her annual donation to the JCR accordingly.

∞

He shuffled willingly into the past on the heels of two ancient aristocrats, the Princesse de X and the Comte de Y, who had known Proust in his fashionable days. Auriol Anders had tracked them down and persuaded them to face the cameras and describe their personal relationships with the author as part of the celebrations to commemorate his birth on 10 July one hundred years ago.

The reconstruction of the dining-room of the Grand Hotel, Balbec, in the Proust Museum in London enchanted Bar-Lev. It took him back at once to the last occasion he had visited the hotel in Cabourg upon which the fictional Grand Hotel was modelled. It was summer, 1920. Proust had wished to return to the scenes of his childhood and had invited Bar-Lev and their friend Chaim Saul-Dubrovsky.

While they dined Marcel had pointed out to his guests that a hotel was much like a permanent set in a provincial theatre. Like that of a provincial theatre, the hotel set remained constant whatever the production – comedy, farce, tragedy or operetta – that unfolded before it. Scanning the dining-room, Marcel had observed that every piece of furniture down to the stiff white damask and sparkling crystal and silver that garnished the tables was identical to that of his childhood. In those days, so far off, the 'production' had been domestic comedy at which he had been both participant and spectator. On the occasion Bar-Lev was remembering he,

Marcel and Chaim had felt themselves to be spectators only. But Marcel's attention was fixed on the troupe of waiters whom he likened to the Israelites of Racine's chorus in *Athalie* and it was not long before all three felt themselves as much on the threshold of the Temple of Solomon as on that of a prodigious meal.

It was the memory of how Marcel directed himself and his two companions in their roles as spectators and participants that brought Bar-Lev to the details of Marcel's quest. He revealed to the astonished company how Marcel had involved himself in the degradation of *Maman* and recounted the excesses he had indulged in in his determination to restore the soul of his mother to the Godhead. Both as spectator at theatrical orgies he directed and as participant in many, Marcel re-enacted the sexual atrocities of history and invented many more. His audience was held spellbound.

Miss Gluckstein had not been present at the recording and was unaware of the furore that her charge had created – as he himself appeared to be – when she got him and his small case on to the Paris train.

'Let me know when to meet you,' she said kindly, handing him a carrier bag with food for the journey. When the train drew out of Victoria Station Miss Gluckstein saw before her a little vacation. She felt liberated of something irritating, even unpleasant, that had been hovering over her these past few days. As a little celebration she burst out of the straitjacket of her usual frugality and bought a bunch of scabious for herself from the flower-seller in Victoria Street.

∞

Spoltz had been largely destroyed in World War II. In the absence of their menfolk the Polish women had abandoned their stricken village and joined up with the peasants in isolated farmsteads as rumours of the Russian advance reached their ears.

When in 1945 the concentration camps were liberated a handful of half-crazed Jews obstinately refused offers of resettlement abroad and, in accordance with vows made in the camps, made their way back to Spoltz in the forlorn hope of rejoining family and friends. A community of some twenty Jewish men and women combined to reinstate one of the squares of houses in the deserted village, and with money provided by American well-wishers bought cattle and seed.

Before long Polish farmers living four miles from Spoltz noticed activity on the land around the village. They investigated. As a result of their investigation they spoke to other farmers at the monthly cattle market in Zorinskaya and, to the accompaniment of much vodka-swilling, joined to lament the failure of the Germans' much vaunted efficiency.

'How come they didn't get rid of the lot?'

It was not clear how many farmers volunteered to finish the work the Germans had left undone. A small band of them rode into Spoltz at night. They located the farm machinery; some they loaded on to a cart, other pieces they wheeled away. They rounded up the cattle and drove them out of the village. The Jews must have sensed what was to be their fate. The men tried to bar the farmers from entering their houses and were felled behind their doors. The women were garrotted in their beds. All living trace of the survivors of Auschwitz was wiped out. With the main objective of their journey accomplished, the farmers set fire to the square of reinstated houses which, being constructed of wood, they razed with a single box of matches. However, attempts to destroy the last vestiges of the sacred buildings failed. They had been partially rebuilt in stone and brick.

∞

There was no reason why Lev should have recognized Warsaw railway station. He had been there only once, when he was ten and very sad. But the sound of the Polish language drove him back to a life he seemed to own, a life more intimately his than the one he had acquired in exile. The thick necks, square heads and gross torsos of those he saw aroused in him first distaste and then fear. It was the fear that was peculiarly familiar; for more than sixty years he had been harbouring that fear within him, lodged in a corner of his being waiting for something to ignite it and set him to flight. And now it was the language that was activating it – and the uniforms, so many uniforms. Were they police? Or were they military?

Lev enquired at the Information Office. The train for Zorinskaya would leave from Platform 6, in half an hour. It was the Gdansk train.

Lev knew the Gdansk train stopped at Zorinskaya once a week. Miss Gluckstein had acquired this piece of information in London and noted it down for him. The piece of paper was in his hand. He boarded the train and sat down on a corner seat. He showed no interest in his surroundings but immediately buried himself in a book, nor did he look up from his book until he heard over the loudspeaker that the train was drawing in to Zorinskaya. As he descended the steps and dropped on to the platform he was somewhat surprised to find himself the sole passenger alighting. On his map the station appeared to serve the countryside for many miles about, yet he was alone on the platform. The guard threw down a number of packages and blew his whistle and the train pulled out, leaving a profound silence and desolation.

The train had rounded a corner and was well lost from view by the time a young man ambled on to the platform to take charge of the goods. Lev approached him, showed him his ticket and asked him how to get to Spoltz.

'Spoltz? Never heard of it. It's not round here!'

'It's to the east. About ten miles' distance.'

'Well, if you say so . . .'

'Is there a bus?'

'A bus?' The young man's voice rose in an official sneer.

Lev, taking his directions from the sun, which was blazing hot at two in the afternoon, walked east along the only road that lay outside the small station. He was accustomed to walking long distances and the ten miles before him would take no more than three hours – probably less, he thought. But he was hot. He stopped at a stile, removed his jacket and took from the now torn carrier bag a sandwich, an apple, and his map. He rested comfortably, his back against the stile, looking about him, consulting the map. There was no breeze; the rye stood at attention. Beside the rye there lay a field of emerald brassicas and to the side of them purple leaves of beet. A pair of flamboyant butterflies mated on the wing, hurling themselves against the red cover of his map. Rooks cackled in the elms, and a lone hawk circled overhead, suddenly swooping low to scavenge. But there appeared to be no humankind abroad; as far as the eye could see or the ear could hear all human life was absent. As Lev took in the scene he recognized nothing particular and yet all seemed familiar. He did not recognize the contours of the land. Why should he? He had never passed this way before. Yet all else rhymed perfectly with his memories: the crops that lay contentedly side by side, the variety of flowers and shrubs that constituted the hedgerows, the lean of the elms bent by Siberian blasts. And, as he shaded his eyes and looked out on to the horizon, the farm buildings.

It was just as he had located the buildings that he heard horse's hooves and the noise of sparking metal. A horse and cart was approaching carrying milk churns. When the old woman driving the horse spotted Lev she tightened the reins and ordered the animal to halt.

'Are you going far?' she asked, as Lev pulled himself on to the bench beside her.

'You are not from here about,' she observed. No, Lev agreed, he was not. But he chose not to elaborate. The old woman scanned him closely. She was reassured. He spoke Polish, he was as old as she, and he had touched his hat to her.

'Where are you bound for?'

'Spoltz!'

'Spoltz!' Her surprise was accompanied by disdain. 'Oh! Spoltz!...' She fell silent. But as her silence deepened she urged the horse to go faster. For two miles she did not speak and then she set Lev down, saying she was turning off the road here but he should walk straight on, although she, herself, could see no good reason for visiting Spoltz.

There were four more miles to walk. As Lev trudged on he wondered about the old woman. She was his age; she had lived her life, no doubt, just four miles from Spoltz. What part had she played in its history?

Bar-Lev was approaching Spoltz from the road that had once been an exclusively Polish thoroughfare, the one along which sugar beet was carted. A single crumbling brick wall, held together by a stout ivy-root, was all that was left of the beet warehouse. Bar-Lev left the road to investigate, his feet stumbling over rubble concealed under the long grass. He climbed back on to the road and walked on. Two hundred yards further and he round himself at a crossroads. The crossroads! Instinctively, he turned left. He was walking down his road, to his home. His pace quickened. He left the road and under a rash of stinging nettles covered in dust (scattered by the wind that swept unimpeded over the flat, featureless land), he could feel the shards of the houses of the Jews. Bar-Lev stood in the graveyard of family life, on the graves of homes. He looked about him, seeing nothing, consumed by pain. He felt himself sway. He dropped his head and tried to bend at the waist. His brain needed blood. He raised himself, and his eyes fastened on two crumbling walls across the way. all that remained of the synagogue. As the sound of clanging bells made vivid the silence of the Llandornic valley so the crumbling walls of the synagogue completed the desolation of Spoltz.

Bar-Lev dragged himself across to the synagogue walls and, climbing over piles of scattered bricks, hauled himself on to a ledge, all that remained of the floor. It was here, at the east wall, that his father had prayed along with the most respected Jews of Spoltz. The east wall was a place of privilege and when his father had been denied access to the synagogue he had suffered a double humiliation: he could no longer count himself among the wise, or among the religious. Bar-Lev stood with his back resting against the hallowed wall. Sixty years ago the Ark would have been at his side and all about him, bobbing, a sea of black and white as the men tricked out in phylacteries and prayer shawls adhered to the prohibitions and rededicated themselves to a God the worship of whom took their minds off their poverty and gave them the sense of identity from which, in time, only their persecutors would benefit.

Lev closed his eyes. Love and indignation filled the places vacated by pain. He was determined to suspend judgement. He opened his eyes to the west, he thrust out his arms and he cried out: 'YISGADAL VA-YISKADASH SHEMAY RABAH.' The words rose out of him like boiling lava. They had always been there, dormant, and now they erupted in a violent steady flow. He chanted loudly, his words filling the air within the walls and echoing outside in the developing dusk. They reached into every corner of the ruined ghetto. Bar-Lev sensed the presence of Jewish ghosts rising gratefully to his words. And when he had delivered his prayer he sank back exhausted against the vestiges of wall: he needed its support. But the wall was older and more infirm than he and could not be relied upon for support. First, one or two bricks fell inward, then one or two fell outward. Bar-Lev listened as the bricks thudded to the ground. The weak wall was gently bulging outward and bricks were toppling from its narrow summit. The old man threw out his arms.

'SHEMA YISROEL!' he bellowed.

'SHEMA YISROEL!' The words echoed round the ruined synagogue, theirs the only sound, the only movement. Bar-Lev lay flattened under the weight of the east wall with the words of affirmation on his lips. He had come home. He was dead.

Family Relations

YAKOV MANDELBAUM'S WORKING DAY was over, a fact for which he thanked the God in whom he did not believe. All the while he picked his way through the rotting debris in Spitalfields Market he focused on the ground, scanning the gutters. At last he fell upon an unblemished apple and two almost unbruised carrots. Into an interior monologue couched in hopelessness he inserted these finds, and for a split second his mood lightened. There was the prospect of a little pleasure to come, something fresh to eat in the dark of the night.

Because he spoke only a few words of English, there was nothing but the meanest work for Yakov and he was grateful to Mendle, the glazier, for taking him on to do his deliveries. All the English needed for the job was a shrill 'mindyerbacks'. On the other hand Yakov could have done with a more robust physique. It was exhausting labour for anyone, but much more so for a man with his lack of muscle and stature. He trudged the streets of Whitechapel bent double to prevent the frame he carried with the sheets of glass scraping the ground and risk shattering them. Now freed of his burden for the day, he made an effort to stretch. His muscles could not respond.

Tired, dirty, hungry and thirsty he dragged himself into his tenement yard. Lowering his face under the tap he drank a long draught. Then he sat trying to get his breath back before filling the bucket chained to the post and stripping off his shirt to wash.

If Yakov recognized himself in his fatigue, his pallor, his unassuaged hunger and his filth, it was the stench that spoke Whitechapel to him. The air was thick with chicken swill. Clouds of smoke gushed from the chimney stacks and merged with soot from the railway line. Decaying leather and the hair of dead animals wafted from factory gates to meet the stink of lavatories and rubbish bins. The stench of the outside was augmented by the stench from the inside, that of clothes soaked in urine and sweat that might never be removed but always be worn stuck to the skin. The ubiquitous odours of cooking that started alluringly and whetted his appetite quickly turned sour in the general mix of smells. This alliance freighted Yakov's lungs, making them thick and heavy, and his gorge heave.

With difficulty he mounted the four flights of stairs to his room. His legs were jelly and he was still breathless. He must negotiate the treads carefully, for many were rotten. The tenement was not only crumbling, infested and dark, it was dangerously overcrowded. He counted the number of tenants as he passed each door. The rapacious landlord was putting families of seven – two adults and five children – in two rooms with a tap, telling them to be grateful not to have to go down to the yard for every drop of water they needed, like everyone else.

Yakov owed the good fortune of a room to himself to Mendle's misfortune. Most single men doubled up, one working days, the other nights. The bed never aired, it remained animal-warm from the previous occupant. But Mendle needed more money than the demand for glass provided. He cleared his daughters out of the little back room and into the kitchen, where the family ate and his wife slept under the table, and himself into the second room with the boys. Yakov got his own seven feet by four overlooking a sunless yard.

He could afford only one meal a day. He took it at the Polish café in Brick Lane. Beyle Krasnastaw cooked recognizably Polish food and served it piping hot at modest prices. He kept open three hundred and sixty-two days a year.

English was rarely heard within those four walls. Men from Poland, most of whom had arrived in Whitechapel a generation or two before Yakov, met to talk of old times over lemon tea. They were hungry for accounts of more recent goings-on. They read the papers, they were appalled. They wanted first-hand experiences. In this Yakov disappointed. He did not come from any of the centres of Jewish habitation – Warsaw or Lvov – where terror reigned. He came from a village some days' horse and cart ride from any large town.

He was a born and bred country boy, reliant upon fresh air and fresh food. He had taken over his father's beasts and vegetable plot when the old man died. He carried on as his father had and sold his livestock and vegetables from the market. He had a few friends there but at thirty was still unmarried. He satisfied his lust every ten or fourteen days in a neighbouring village with a gentile girl.

Yakov had no reason to believe that his gentile neighbours would not remain as indifferent to his Jewishness as they had been to his father's. But times were changing. Tensions were mounting. The younger generation, the church and particularly a local family jealous of his unmortgaged land recognized a climate sympathetic to Jew-baiting. His existence became threatened. His girl told him that Jews in neighbouring towns were having to flee if they were to escape forced labour in Germany. Yakov was in something of a quandary. He loved the house and land, but he was not going to work for the Germans. One night he lifted the floor-boards in the kitchen, removed his savings, harnessed the horse and rode away.

He had been in England almost a year, expecting friends to have joined him to set up somewhere together. But none had come. Nor had he received news from them. His money, which had seemed quite substantial, had run out and his wage only covered his room and meal. It could have been so much easier, he thought, had his friends joined him. They would have pooled their resources. The first thing they would have done is get out of the tenement. Living there was like living in crumbling cheese. The walls were friable with the sounds of Yiddish being shouted in exchanges from one room to the next, one floor to the next, one building to the next. Yakov wondered where these women learned to shout? It seemed the entire population had forgotten how to talk. From open windows where women sat bent double over sewing machines, shrieks exploded from mothers scolding their children and wives abusing their worthless husbands. All roared with fury against the injustices of the world. Passing mean buildings of unlit rooms Yakov heard other passionate arguments in progress: men in skull-caps disputing the precise meaning of a passage of law promulgated five thousand years ago, in a far-flung country.

He threaded his way through the little groups of unemployed men gathered to share their anguish. He should be grateful for his job. But he wondered, did Mendle only give it to him because no other man would put up with so mean a wage? It was a relief to find his corner at Krasnastaw's unoccupied. And it was quiet in the café. The men laid aside the sheets of the Yiddish paper they shared as soon as Beyle served their food. Such sounds as arose were ones of contented lapping and chewing. Yakov bent over the hot, fat, greasy dumpling in the paprika stew. He looked forward to the lemon tea being served and the murmur of men whispering their dreams starting up.

But Yakov's close attention to his dumpling stew was interrupted by the unexpected presence of Beyle Krasnakaw at his elbow.

'Someone's bin looking for you.'

'Polish?'

'Yes.' Yakov felt faint with joy. Someone from his village had arrived at last.

'Gave her your address. Reckoned you'd not mind a lovely young lady having it.'

'Lady?' Yakov's initial pleasure was disturbed. He felt uneasy. No woman not already condemned to life in a tenement in Whitechapel should seek him out there. 'When's she coming back?' he asked Beyle.

'Dunno. Didn't say.'

Yakov considered returning to his room forthwith, but rejected the notion in favour of finishing his stew. Then he put off the unknown still further by drawing up his chair, where four regulars sat, and speculating with them who his visitor could be. He didn't know any Polish *women* who would be seeking him out. The visitor hadn't left her name. Obviously, that must be because he wouldn't recognize it.

He strolled back, savouring expectation. On his way to his room he knocked on Mendle's door. 'Anyone been asking for me?' he asked as nonchalantly as he could manage. Peering over Mendle's shoulder he caught sight of a young woman dressed in a light, cool dress. She was sitting with Mendle's youngest on her knee. He recognized the blond hair at once. It was Danny! Mrs Mendle was shouting above the noise of her two battling boys, listing the advantages of life in England while Danny, Yakov's cousin, quietly absorbed the disadvantages evident all about her.

'Danny!' Yakov gasped. Mrs Mendle grabbed back the baby. Danny stood and stared at her cousin. They had not seen one another since the death of Danny's father, six years back in Warsaw. He scratched himself vigorously. The ever-hungry fleas, provoked by his sweat, were making a meal of him.

Danny took her leave so graciously of Mr and Mrs Mendle, thanking them for having asked her in while she waited for Yakov. Yakov had forgotten that such manners existed. Since being condemned to Whitechapel tenement life, other worlds had receded beyond his imaginative horizon. Seeing his exquisite cousin, dressed elegantly in such bleak surroundings, only emphasized to Yakov the depths to which he felt he had sunk.

Danny asked to go somewhere to talk, alone. Yakov knew he had to take her to his room. His slum appeared the more stinking and derelict for accommodating his cousin's beauty and grace. Yakov was close to tears. He directed Danny up the unlit stairs and threw open his door. He motioned her to take the chair. He sat on the edge of his bed.

First he told her over and over how good it was to see her again, that it was something he had never imagined might happen. No, he reassured her, he was not starving, he had employment. As soon as his friends arrived, he would get out of the tenement. But what was she doing here? Was she going to stay? Danny explained that she had made the journey legally. Because she was taken for Aryan she had obtained an exit visa. She had come to leave a packet of diamonds with Yakov, the value of which would keep her and her husband, Ariel, and enable them to survive in England when she had got him out of Poland. He did not look Aryan. He needed to be smuggled out. She had made the trial run to organize their future escape. She had discovered a safe route and whom to bribe.

She handed two envelopes to Yakov. One contained the diamonds, the other instructions to be followed in the event she did not return. She begged him not to question her further. They sat up all night, Danny's French scent vying with the stench of the tenement. They spoke of family matters, the expropriation of Jewish property, the labour camps, the death camps and the violence in the streets. They knew war was inevitable. Yakov's eyes fixed on Danny's luxuriant blond hair, blue eyes, faultless complexion and voluptuous body. Such physical properties belonged to a world so far away in time and place it seemed never to have existed.

He begged Danny not to return to Poland. Surely, Ariel could find his own way out? But Danny knew otherwise. She told Yakov of the people who were disappearing off the streets of Warsaw. She had seen the destruction of Jewish shops and the stoning of mere children. Tots. Her passport was her Aryan appearance and her husband must travel on it, too. When they got back to London there would be money enough for the three of them to live on. Yakov must have confidence. Just a few more weeks...

Danny never did return. When the war was over. Yakov learned that she and Ariel had been caught *en route* to England and taken to Auschwitz and gassed. Yakov lived out the war in Whitechapel. He never made any money but he did manage to move into less damp and dirty rooms with his own (cold) water tap. He took English lessons and started to educate himself.

Initially, the diamonds had posed a problem for him. There was nowhere safe to stash them. He made himself a little pouch which he wore round his waist for the duration. Once the authorities at Woburn House had been able to confirm the deaths of Danny and Ariel, Yakov opened the other envelope and read the instructions Danny had left. The diamonds were to be delivered to an address in Holland Park.

Unknown to Yakov, Sir Albert Gordon of Holland Park was a relative, one to whom a member of the Warsaw branch of the family owed a sum of money. The debt had been incurred some thirty years past. Time and the pressure of the holocaust might have been expected to wipe out such a matter. They hadn't. In the event, Yakov on his second attempt to gain access to the occupants had been sent round to the tradesmen's entrance, his appearance having been relayed to her employer by the parlourmaid.

Sir Albert received Yakov in his study. He did not offer

him a seat. He took the letter and the envelope containing the diamonds and thanked Yakov for both. He sat down behind his desk and having read the letter poured the diamonds on to the desk top and counted them. He paused, mentally calculating their value. Then he rumbled under his jacket, and withdrew his wallet from the inside pocket. He extracted four five pound notes and handed them to Yakov. 'Corruption wins not more than honesty,' he quoted patting Yakov on the back and simultaneously pressing a bell. The parlourmaid appeared and showed Yakov out of the house.

ALSO AVAILABLE FROM ARCADIA BOOKS

Tomorrow
Elisabeth Russell Taylor

August 1960: a number of ill-assorted guests have gathered at The Tamarisks, a small hotel on the Danish island of Møn. Among them is Elisabeth Danziger, plain, middle-aged and unobtrusive, a woman so utterly predictable in her habits that she has come to the island every summer for the past fifteen years.

Elisabeth comes back to remember. For the seven days of her holiday, she will permit the past to haunt her with happy memories of growing up on the island in a brilliant and gifted family – but also with darker thoughts, over which she must struggle to achieve control.

As she follows her never-changing itinerary, Elisabeth has no reason to suspect that this year will be any different from the others...

'Elisabeth Russell Taylor's spare, subtle evocations of menace, abuse and psychic tragedy are interwoven with a profound spiritual integrity. Unjustly neglected, she is entirely original and wholly brilliant'
– Elizabeth Young

'A haunting, beautifully written lament for the isolating power of love' – *Financial Times*

'Full of precise observations and unexpected lines ... A melancholy, compelling book with a surprising ending' – *Observer*

'Beautiful, haunting ... Elisabeth Russell Taylor portrays a poignant betrayal of grief and failed communication' – Zoé Fairbairns

'A memorable and poignant novel made all the more heartbreaking by the quiet dignity of its central character and the restraint of its telling'
– Shena Mackay

ALSO AVAILABLE FROM ARCADIA BOOKS

Present Fears
Elisabeth Russell Taylor

'A sparkling collection of stories, each with a sting in its tail. They give no comfort, but provoke thought and may leave you lamenting the lost opportunities that thwart so many lives'
– *Sunday Times*

'Elegant and witty surfaces break open to reveal the darkness at the heart of these cosmopolitan tales' – Georgina Hammick

'Outstanding . . . the people described here should be fitted with a danger sign. At any moment their surface control may crack. Excellent entertainment' – *Mail on Sunday*

'An exceptional début collection which proves that a sharp eye and clear voice still carry more weight than loud, cheap thrills. The lurid and engaging precision of her style is reminiscent of Austen and almost as robust as Fielding. A rare treat that impresses on the first reading and – even more unusual – improves on the second.'
– *Kirkus Reviews*

'It is hard to pinpoint what makes these stories so unsettling. Their worlds – some border territory between genteel suburbia and dreamland – are imagined with an eerie thoroughness. The inhabitans are all out of kilter, and terrifyingly fragile; spinstering middle-agers paralysed by sexual fear; anxious children in the centre of parental power games. Taylor's abrupt, elegantly engineered anticlimaxes leave the reader with the disquieting feeling of waiting for the other shoe to fall' – *Observer*

'The writing is not only elegantly flexed but also funny . . . there is a warmth in fact throughout the book that makes the ice of its lives more moving, rather than less' – *Times Literary Supplement*

'Witty, deadpan language with a bleakness reminiscent of Roald Dahl' – *Daily Telegraph*

'Excellent entertainment' – *Mail on Sunday*

ALSO AVAILABLE FROM ARCADIA BOOKS

The Twins
Tessa de Loo

Translated from the Dutch by Ruth Levitt

Two elderly women, one Dutch and one German, meet by chance at the famous health resort of Spa. They recognize in the other their twin sister they believed to be lost. They begin to tell each other their life stories, the last chance to bridge a gulf of almost seventy years.

Born in Cologne in 1916, the twins are brusquely separated from each other after the death of their parents. Anna grows up with her grandfather, in a primitive farming and Catholic milieu on the edge of the Teutoburgerwald. Lotte ends up in the Netherlands because of her TB, living with an uncle who harbours strong socialist sympathies. Bad relationships between the families and the intervening war cause the contact between the two sisters to be broken. When their paths cross again so late in life, Lotte, who sheltered Jews in hiding during the war, is initially extremely suspicious of her newly-found twin sister. But through Anna's painful stories she is confronted with the other side of her own reality: the sufferings of ordinary Germans in wartime.

In this monumental novel, Tessa de Loo compellingly weaves the story of two twin sisters separated in childhood with that of two countries opposed in war, and depicts, in a simple yet harrowing prose the effects of nature and nurture on the individual.

'All-seeing, it is brimming with scenes that are moving and sometimes disturbing' – *Der Spiegel*

'A magnificent book. It reveals a kaleidoscope in which drama, comedy, farce and poetry combine to create a novel that must be read' – *Die Woche*

ALSO AVAILABLE FROM ARCADIA BOOKS

His Mistress's Voice
Gillian Freeman

'Jews! Murderers! Killers of Christ!' There was no problem of interpretation. A small group of men and women, sombre in black, children amongst them, shouted abuse as the immigrants were jostled towards the gates, still being harried for their custom...

Victorian England: Simon, a young Jewish widower with a small son emigrates from Warsaw to London's East End, staying with his sister and her family until he takes up the position of cantor at a smart Reform synagogue off Lower Regent Street. His liaison with Phoebe Fenelle, a leading actress of the day, leads to dire consequences for her husband, a major in the Royal Household Cavalry – or does it?

In her tenth and most powerful novel to date, Gillian Freeman vividly recreates the London theatre world of the day and counterpoises this life of frivolity and artifice with the position of Jews – both rich and poor – in the wider society.

'A serious, touching book, unpretentiously powerful. The images are haunting, indelible' – Robert Altman

'A very unusual and original story, entertainingly and carefully observed. The period is uncannily evoked, and has something of the frisson of a Henry James ghost story' – *Financial Times*

'Lively, evocative and satisfyingly tangled' – *Sunday Telegraph*

'Ingenious ... what seems at first to be an entertainment turns into a very good, even moving, novel' – *The Times*

'She writes with uncommon ease and emancipation' – *Guardian*

'Her writing is pure pleasure' – *Evening Standard*

ARCADIA BOOKS
are available from all good bookshops
or direct from the publishers at 15–16 Nassau Street, London W1N 7RE.
Write for a free catalogue.